Brian Boru
Emperor of the Irish

Morgan Llywelyn

TOR®

A Tom Doherty Associates Book
New York

BRIAN BORU: EMPEROR OF THE IRISH

Copyright © 1990 by Morgan Llywelyn

A Tor Book
Published by Tom Doherty Associates, Inc.
175 Fifth Avenue
New York, NY 10010

Tor® is a registered trademark of Tom Doherty Associates, Inc.

Design by Lynn Newmark

ISBN: 0-812-54461-7
Library of Congress Card Catalog Number: 95-6318

First published by The O'Brien Press
First Tor edition: June 1995
First Tor mass market edition: October 1997

Printed in the United States of America

0 9 8 7 6 5 4 3 2 1

CONTENTS

LIST OF NAMES

Some of the names from this period of Irish history are unpronounceable by non-Gaelic speakers. We have presented them in a form as close as possible to the original sound but easily spoken by readers of English. Here we list the names that have been altered, with their original spelling. Other names have been altered simply by history, and we have used the now-common versions of these names (Brian, Kennedy).

Achra—Eachraidh
Aval—Aoibheall
Bebinn—Béibionn
Brian Boru—Brian Boramha (or, Sive— Sadhbh in later Irish, Ború)
Callahan—Ceallacháin
Carroll—Cearbhaill
Conor—Conchobhair
Donal—Domhnall
Donncha—Donnchadh
Ducholi—Dubhchobhlaigh
Edigan—Éideagáin

Gormla—Gormlaith
Hugh—Aodh
Kennedy—Cinnéide
Maelmora—Maelmórdha
Mahon—Mathgamhain
Malachy—Maolseachlainn
Marcan—Marcán
Mor—Mór
Murcha—Murchadh
Teige—Tadhg
Tomas—Tomás

Clans
Dalcassians—Dál gCais

O'Neills—Uí Néill
Owenacht—Eoghanacht

Places
Glenn Mauma—Gleann
  Máma
Kincora—Ceann Córadh

Other
banshee—bean sí
shanachy—seanachaí
  (storyteller)
shee—sí (fairies, ''little
  people'')

ONE

Descended from Kings

The river ran on forever. Night and day it called to him, "Come away with me and see what lies beyond the mountains!"

Brian was surrounded by mountains. Behind the fort where he had been born rose the mighty Slieve Bernagh. There the guardian spirit of his tribe, the banshee known as Aval, watched over them from her brooding gray crag. Across the river and to the south were more mountains. But the Shannon escaped them all. She ran on and on to places the boy could only dream about.

"Take me with you," he whispered sometimes.

Brian mac Kennedy was the youngest of a dozen sons born to a prince of the Dalcassian tribe, rulers of the land of Thomond in the province of Munster.

The sons of Kennedy and his wife Bebinn were a rowdy, brawling lot. Mahon was Brian's favorite. Mahon was broad and strong and could always find time to wink at his youngest brother or rumple his red-gold hair.

It was Mahon who taught Brian how to make snares to catch small game, and how to whistle. When they were together Brian felt warm inside and very brave, walking in his tall brother's shadow.

"Tell me a story," he would say.

He never tired of listening to tales of the great kings and the endless battles that were fought between the kingdoms of Ireland. Munster, Leinster, Connacht, Meath, Ulster—each had its heroes. A king protected his people and seized the land and cattle of other kings, and shared his wealth with his supporters.

"If I were a king," Brian boasted, "every person in my kingdom would grease his knife with fat meat every day."

Mahon laughed. "Would they now? And would you be a fine fierce warrior with a gold torc around your neck?" He loved his youngest brother, who already showed promise of the strong man he would become. It's a pity Brian will never be a king, thought Mahon, watching him, because he's going to look like one.

Sometimes, when Brian gazed toward the mountains or the river, his gray eyes held the faraway look of an eagle.

But he was still a ten-year-old boy and full of mischief. He could usually convince his older brothers, who should have known better, to take part. Once he persuaded them to take their father out hunting every day for a fortnight, leaving a few of Kennedy's favorite hounds behind to guard the ring fort on the west bank of the Shannon.

While Kennedy was away, Brian taught the hounds to howl loudly at a signal from himself.

The signal was a high, thin whistle, blown through a leaf of grass. A blow to the head from a Danish battle ax had left Kennedy somewhat deaf, so he could not hear it, but his hounds could. Once he had trained the dogs to respond, Brian hid himself near the gate of the fort and waited for his father's return.

The moment Kennedy entered Beal Boru the hounds began to howl. The sound echoed around and around the circular earthen walls of the fort, which were reinforced with stone and topped by a timber palisade. The noise was awful.

Kennedy was very upset. "I don't understand this!" he kept saying. "My hounds love me, they always run to lick my hands when I come home. Why are they howling this time?"

Whenever there was trouble, Bebinn looked for her youngest son. While the hounds were still crying, she caught sight of Brian hiding in the shadows. His eyes were sparkling and he had his hand over his mouth to keep from laughing out loud.

Bebinn's lips twitched with their own desire to

laugh, but she made herself say sternly, "Brian, calm the dogs, will you? And you, husband, come into the house and sit by the fire. There is mead waiting."

She led Kennedy into their house—a circular timber lodge in the center of the fort, with a roof of thatch made from river reeds and a stone firepit in the middle of the flagstone floor. Meat was roasting on the spit. The smell of the crackling fat, and a cup of mead or honey wine, would soon make Kennedy forget the strange behavior of his hounds.

At the door Bebinn looked back over her shoulder. "You cause more trouble than the rest of them put together in a basket," she said to her youngest son.

But Brian knew she was not really angry. She was never really angry with any of her children, unlike Kennedy, whose face could turn red with rage. Bebinn had a soft center. She was tender and good-humored and endlessly patient.

Brian followed Mahon everywhere he could, but he always came back to Bebinn. She was home; she was the heart of his world.

When the hounds were quiet at last—and his brothers were still laughing at the joke—Brian left the fort as he often did to wander along the path beside the river. He loved being surrounded by his happy, noisy family, but he also wanted to be alone sometimes too.

He stood for a while, staring at the silvery water. Then he turned and looked up toward the gray crag to the west. "Aval, are you watching?" he wanted to know. "Do you see me now?"

Sometimes he thought he could feel her eyes on him. The sensation was curiously comforting. Aval was magic, one of the Old People whom the priests spoke out against, but even the priests did not condemn them too loudly. Everyone knew that the power of the ancient gods could still be felt in Ireland, in the hills and streams and thorn trees, in the great, silent mounds into which they had vanished so long ago. The shee!

Brian tossed a salute to Aval on her lonely crag.

Sometimes, when his family visited the abandoned homestead below the crag that had belonged to Brian's grandfather Lorcan, Brian slipped away from the others and left a small offering of food for Aval. You could never tell; it might be wise. Just in case.

Once his mother saw him do it, and nodded. "I have brought gifts to her myself," she told Brian as they were scrambling back down the hill together, pushing through the heather and bracken.

Now Brian stared toward the crag and wondered why the priests did not like the shee. Had not one creator made them all? Someday he would have to ask someone about that.

A trumpet sounded from the fort, breaking into his thoughts. He forgot about rivers and banshees. The trumpet meant the main meal of the day was ready, and young Brian was always hungry.

He spun around and raced for home, licking his

lips. With his brothers, he crowded into the lodge, bringing into its smoky interior the smells of fresh air and open fields. Each member of the family was served in turn, according to his rank. Such strict traditions were always observed, not only among the warrior nobility but in the poorest sod huts of the leather tanners and stone breakers. Status was very important; it told everyone where a person stood in relation to his or her clan, tribe, and kingdom. Each rank had its entitlements under the ancient Brehon law. As the son of a Dalcassian prince, Brian would be entitled to receive an education from the monks when he was older, as his brothers had before him.

"Don't grab!" one of those brothers now snarled as Brian's hunger overcame him and he reached for food out of turn. "There's enough for everyone, Brian, just wait."

There *was* enough for everyone. In the tenth century of the Christian era, Ireland was a land of plenty as it had always been. Cattle thrived on the rich grasslands, and there was always game to be hunted. Beef and pork and mutton were eaten often, but also venison, badger, squirrel, wildfowl, and even seal meat near the coasts, as well as many varieties of fish and shellfish. Soft fruits and cheeses were summer foods, served with kale and cresses and great chunks of dark bread dipped in bowls of buttermilk. In the winter, people ate nuts, and root vegetables like parsnips and turnips, as well as sausages and puddings and more bread thickly smeared with butter and dripping. Even the poorest need not go hungry in Ireland, which provided enough for all her children.

On this evening the meal included the usual summer foods, as well as roasted woodcock, a broth of mushrooms and barley, and balls of suet rolled in honey and pine nuts.

Bebinn kept a sharp eye on her children as they ate. Kennedy was only the ruler of a local tribe, but his wife was a princess of Connacht, a daughter of the provincial king, Murcha. She demanded that her sons observe royal manners. They must hold their knives properly in their right hands, tearing off bits of food with the fingers of the left hand, and when he had finished eating each boy must wipe his hands on one of his mother's linen napkins, a treasure she had brought with her to her marriage.

"You are not savages," she was fond of reminding them. "You are descended from kings."

"From kings," young Brian would whisper to himself, as if the words held a promise.

TWO

Plundered!

The longships came nosing through the mist that lay thick on the river. Their prows were ferocious wooden dragon heads, painted in the colors of fire and blood. They struck terror into the hearts of the Irish. Wherever the rivers flowed, the foreigners from the cold lands, the Danes and the Norsemen, sailed up them to pillage and plunder.

The foreigners called it "going viking."

For as long as he could remember, Brian had heard terrible stories of Viking raids. When Kennedy's family sat around the fire at night, and the old shanachy of the Dalcassians told tales of blood and death, young Brian felt a delicious shiver of fear.

But it did not last long. He could always shrug it

off by imagining himself as a mighty hero with a sword, driving the Vikings away. All his brothers would crowd around him and praise him, instead of teasing him because he was the youngest. And Bebinn would give him extra lumps of honeyed suet as a treat. •

The threat of the Vikings did not seem real to him. He had never seen a Viking raid; it was just a story the tribe's storyteller told to pass the long winter nights.

But then the longships came nosing up the Shannon.

At the time, Brian was with his brothers Mahon and Marcan, tending cattle on the upland meadows some distance from Beal Boru. Marcan, who was dreamy and claimed that God talked to him, was lying on his back chewing a blade of grass and staring at the sky while Mahon was teaching Brian how to watch for threats to the herd. Suddenly he stopped talking and lifted his head, listening. Then he said, "Did you hear that?"

Marcan took the grass out of his mouth. "Hear what?"

Mahon frowned. "Perhaps it was nothing. But I thought . . . there! There it is again!"

The wind had shifted and now all three heard the sound of screams in the distance.

"That's coming from Beal Boru!" Mahon shouted, and began to run, with Brian at his heels. Marcan scrambled to his feet and ran after them, forgetting about the cattle.

The mist in the river valley was too thick. Looking down from the hills, they could not see the fort. But then they caught the first smell of smoke and ran faster.

As they drew near the fort they could hear the crackling of flames and see that the main gate had been torn off its iron hinges. "Stay here!" Mahon ordered Brian as he and Marcan hurried forward.

But Brian did not obey him. Though he loved Mahon, he did not like to take orders from anyone. He trotted through the gateway behind his brothers, then stopped to stare.

He felt the world drop out from under him. Time seemed to stop, leaving him frozen. He could see everything far too clearly, yet he was unable to move.

Every structure inside the fort had been set afire. The main lodge was burning and so were the several outbuildings and smaller lodges for Kennedy's dependents. There was a crash and a huge shower of sparks as a roof collapsed. With a gasp of horror, Brian jumped to one side, only to stumble over the body of the old shanachy. The man was dead and covered with blood.

There were bodies everywhere. One of Brian's brothers lay near the gate, where he had died fighting. Beyond him was a farmer who lived nearby and had fled to the fort for safety, then died there with all his family huddled around him. Brian's shocked eyes saw another of his brothers, with a spear thrust through him, and his mother's favorite milk cow and several of his father's hounds, all slain. Beside them on the earth lay a servant who had helped Bebinn with domestic chores, and then . . .

. . . and then . . .

He tried not to see her. He willed himself not to see her.

Princess Bebinn of Connacht lay in a pool of blood where the Danes had left her.

Brian stumbled forward and fell to his knees beside his mother.

She could not be dead. This was some terrible dream. If only he could open his eyes he would find himself safe and warm in his own bed again, and Bebinn would come at his cry and laugh at him, and hug him, and make everything all right.

He rubbed his eyes with his knuckles. But when he opened them again she still lay on the ground, not moving. There was an awful stillness about her.

Brian felt as if claws were tearing him apart from the inside.

He threw himself across her body and called her again and again, his voice rising until it tore his throat. But he did not feel the pain. The claws inside kept tearing at him until he could feel nothing else.

When he could not bear it any longer he got to his feet and stumbled through the ruins, seeking comfort. Seeing Mahon through tear-filled eyes, Brian ran to him. He threw his arms around Mahon's waist. "Make Mother be all right again!"

he cried. Mahon must do it; he was the big brother who always fixed things.

But Mahon felt as sick and helpless as Brian. This was also his family; his mother and brothers lying dead. He was dazed with shock. He gave Brian's shoulder an absentminded pat but he did not hug the younger boy, or pick him up. He was hardly even aware of him. Instead he left Brian standing where he was and just walked away, shaking his head, fighting back his own tears. At that moment, Mahon had no comfort to spare.

Brian stared after his brother.

Mahon bumped into Marcan without seeing him. Marcan said, "It's a blessing of God that our father was away trading cattle, or he might be lying dead here, too."

"A blessing of God . . ." Mahon repeated the words. The two men looked at each other then, sharing the horror.

Brian watched them from a distance, feeling terribly alone. The worst thing in all the world had happened and there was no one to hold him, no one to hug him and tell him everything would be all right. That was the sort of thing Bebinn would have done. But she would never hug him again.

Never again.

A cold wind seemed to swirl around Brian, chilling him to the marrow. "Mother," he sobbed.

No loving voice answered.

Brian made his way back to Bebinn and sat down beside her, drawing his knees up tight against his chest and wrapping his arms around them. He watched without really seeing as Mahon and Marcan began moving among the bodies, covering faces. Marcan appeared to be saying a prayer over each.

A shout from beyond the gate announced the arrival of another of Kennedy's sons, who had been with a herd beyond Slieve Bernagh. Soon all the surviving members of the family arrived, summoned by the disaster. Each in turn stopped and stared as Brian had done.

Beal Boru was destroyed. Once it had been the proud stronghold of a tribal chieftain who owned many cows. Now it was rubble and ash, containing death.

People seemed to notice Brian only because he was sitting by Bebinn's body. No one knew what to do with him. The women of the clan had been killed or carried off by the Vikings. It had been they who cared for children; men had other work. The only survivors of the family were some of Brian's brothers, men with no experience to equal that of a mother. They were not unkind to Brian, but they did not know what he needed.

Mostly they just left him alone. They had to put out the fires, and collect the dead.

The only time Brian said anything was when they wrapped Bebinn's body in a cloak and carried her away. He followed her with his eyes, saying ''Mother'' just once more.

Very softly.

That night the surviving sons of Kennedy slept together in the ruins of the old homestead below the gray crag. From there, they could not smell the ashes and burnt timber. Other Dalcassians had arrived and offered them help and hospitality, but by mutual agreement they had gone to their grandfather's old fort instead. It was the nearest thing to their destroyed home.

Brian lay on the earth beside Mahon, wrapped in a woolen cloak. He did not think of himself as afraid, but sometimes shudders ran through his body.

A messenger had been sent to find Kennedy, who had gone across the Shannon to arrange a cattle trade with another tribe. When Brian tried, he found he could not remember his father's face. But he could still see his mother as she lay dead.

In the night a shriek wailed down the wind. It was not a human voice.

"It's the banshee," Mahon said, feeling the hairs rise on the back of his neck. "Aval mourns the Dalcassian dead."

No one slept that night, while the voice of the banshee ripped and tore the air.

Rebuilding Beal Boru began as soon as Kennedy returned and the dead were buried. Brian's father was frightening in his anger. At first he hardly spoke to anyone. He broke branches in his rage and drove his fist through burned timber walls. He roared at people in a voice that did not even sound like his own, and Brian stayed as far away from him as he could.

Dalcassians of every rank came to assist their chieftain in rebuilding Beal Boru. Members of the warrior nobility wore gold and silver jewelry and pleated tunics. Freemen who farmed tribal land wore simpler clothing, and servants and unfree laborers dressed in the coarsest homespun, but all worked equally hard. Beal Boru was a symbol of Dalcassian pride.

The surviving members of Kennedy's family were changed by the raid. Kennedy himself was always angry. Marcan now prayed most of the time. Mahon seemed older, quieter, and did not play with Brian anymore.

Brian began starting fights with the sons of nearby farmers. Fighting took his mind off his pain, for a while. He pretended the farmers' sons were Vikings and beat them so savagely their fathers protested to Kennedy.

"I'm sending that young troublemaker away," the chieftain promised. "To the monks at Clonmacnois, for his education."

On the day Brian was to leave for Clonmacnois, his father sent him a set of new clothing, fit for a prince. He was given a linen undershirt with flowing sleeves, and a tunic dyed with saffron, to be belted with carved leather. A new mantle of dark red wool trimmed in otter fur reached almost to the ground, barely revealing snug woolen trousers that extended from his hips to his ankles and were held in place by a strap under the arch of his foot. On Brian's feet were the first shoes he had ever worn, a pair of soft leather boots cut low and embossed with a few strips of silver wire.

He hated the shoes. His feet did not like being trapped in leather; they wanted to feel the earth and the grass.

And the new woolen trousers itched.

When Brian stood before his father for inspection, Kennedy's first words were, "Stop scratching. You'll get used to those trousers."

"Do I really have to go away?" Brian wanted to know. "I want to stay here."

"You're no use to us here. You won't be old enough to take up arms and go to war until you're fifteen, and in the meantime you're in everyone's way. We don't have your mother to mind you now. Going to Clonmacnois is for your own good."

"Whenever someone wants me to do something I don't want to do, they say it's for my own good," Brian protested.

Mahon, who was waiting to take him to the monastic school upriver, chuckled.

Kennedy shot him a warning glance. "Don't encourage the boy; there's too much of the rebel in him already. I don't envy the good brothers who will have to tame him."

Mahon said little on the ride north, and Brian said less. The pain closed around him again. He was being sent away. He had lost his mother; now he was losing his home. He bit his lip and hated the

Vikings. It had all begun with them.

When they arrived at Clonmacnois, the abbot who greeted them looked Brian over from his heels to his head. "What are we to make of you?" he said at last.

"A warrior. I'm going to kill all the Vikings."

"That is not worthy of a Christian," the abbot said sternly. But he gave the boy another look. There was something wild in the young Dalcassian's eyes. This one will be a challenge, the abbot said to himself.

He led the way through a low stone archway into a paved courtyard. A number of scholars were sitting on wooden benches, listening to a monk who was speaking in a strange language.

Brian halted, his eyes narrowing with suspicion. He looked over his shoulder to see what Mahon made of this, but Mahon was gone.

He had left without saying good-bye.

Brian took a deep breath. He was hurt but he would not let it show. I am alone, he thought. Now I have no one but me. He lifted his chin and swallowed hard against the lump in his throat. "What language is that man speaking?" he asked the abbot. "Is he a foreigner?"

"He is teaching Greek," the abbot explained, "which is a tongue, like Latin, that is read by civilized people. But he is as Irish as yourself, born no more than a morning's walk from here."

"Are you going to teach me Greek and Latin?"

"If you are capable of learning them. And if you

are entitled to such an education. What is your ancestry?''

As the historian of the Dalcassians had taught him, Brian recited, ''I am the son of Kennedy who is the son of Lorcan, King of Thomond, who was descended from Corc, first King of Thomond, who was descended from Cormac Cas, and through him from the Milesian princes.''

The abbot nodded. ''You are entitled to all we have to teach, then.''

''Will you train me in the finer arts of sword and spear?'' Brian asked eagerly.

The abbot frowned at him. ''We serve the god of peace here, not the gods of war,'' he said sternly.

But Brian had already noted the high stone walls built to protect the great monastic school that dreamed in the watery meadows beside the Shannon. He had seen the tall stone tower with its cone-shaped roof and asked Mahon about it as they were approaching the place.

''That is a round tower where the monks keep lookout for raiders,'' Mahon had explained. ''If they see Vikings coming up the river, they take the Church's treasures into the top of the tower and pull up the ladder so no one can get to them. It's the only way to protect gold and silver from the Danes and Norsemen . . . and from some of our own plundering clans,'' he had added.

So as he listened to the abbot, Brian was thinking to himself, War comes here in spite of what this man says. There is no safe place, then. But there should be.

There should be!

Brian's early days at Clonmacnois were spent learning the discipline of monastic life. The monks were not gentle teachers. His frequent rebellions were met with frequent punishments, and the rope belt around the abbot's waist was often removed and used across young Brian's back.

In time he became as obedient as he had to be, but they never made him cry. Brian had done his crying at Beal Boru.

When his lessons began he found unexpected pleasure in them. If the weather was fine, classes were taught outside in the courtyards and on the lawns. Most of the students were young men intended for the Church, but some, like Brian, were merely the sons of various noble clans who had been sent to the monks for polishing. From time to time a few well-born girls joined their number to learn to read and write. Under the old Brehon law, education was not denied to women who wanted it.

But the Brehon law itself was not taught at Clonmacnois. As Brother Tomas explained when Brian asked him about it, "The Brehon law is pagan and we are Christian. But we do not openly oppose it, because the people would resist. It is not easy to change a person's beliefs and traditions, Brian, so we have learned to tolerate them, letting the Brehon law exist side by side with Christian teaching. Tolerance is a virtue.''

''Perhaps,'' said Brian, ''but I could never tolerate the foreigners!''

''The young Dalcassian is as prickly as a gorse bush,'' Brother Tomas told the abbot.

To his surprise, Brian discovered that he enjoyed studying. His hungry mind gobbled up information and asked for more. He liked music and mathematics, he was good at languages, but history was best of all. History was filled with war stories, and by studying them he learned how great victories had been won in the past, by heroes far beyond Ireland. Men with names like Alexander and Alfred and Charlemagne. Great warriors all.

By studying how they won, I will learn how the Vikings could be beaten, Brian thought to himself. And when he was poring over his lessons he did not feel so alone.

But he was still only ten years old, and far from home. At night as he lay on his narrow bed in the cold stone dormitory, he hugged himself for comfort and wondered if Aval could still see him. He felt as if he had been torn loose from everything he loved.

At first some of the other students teased him, because he was the youngest pupil in the school. Scholars came from all over Europe to study at Clonmacnois, and a Briton called Alcuin told Brian, ''You spend too much time at your lessons. You will grow soft and fat and become a round-shouldered scribe with weak eyes.''

''Do you think so?'' Brian asked calmly. He was half afraid of Alcuin, who was larger and older, but he would not let the fear show. Fear was like crying—no one must see. Setting aside his wax tablet and pointed stylus, he fell upon Alcuin with doubled fists.

Brian was winning when the monks finally pulled them apart.

The abbot was not pleased. ''How are we to cure you of this fighting?'' he asked, almost in despair.

''I am a warrior,'' Brian said stubbornly.

''You are still a child!''

That night the rope lashed Brian's back, but he did not cry out. The next day, Alcuin came to him and offered to be friends.

One by one, the other students became his friends too. They liked and admired Brian, who appeared both cheerful and fearless. They could not see how he felt inside and he kept it to himself. It was wonderful to be part of a group again, to have companions who laughed and joked with him— and looked up to him.

For, to the great surprise of the abbot, in time Brian proved to be the best scholar at Clonmacnois.

But sometimes he wandered away from his friends and walked alone beside the Shannon, his eyes following the water as if it were a road leading south to Beal Boru.

''I will go back,'' he promised himself, ''and use what I have learned here to build the strongest fortress in Ireland and be revenged on the foreigners!''

Action was one answer to pain and grief. Learning was another. Learning opened up the world to Brian, and when the bell sounded he left the river and returned to the classroom to study the career of Charlemagne of France, who had dreamed great dreams and made them come true.

THREE

Becoming a Warrior

There was always more to learn. When one of the monks from Clonmacnois traveled south to the monastic school of Inisfallen, amid the lakes of Killarney, Brian traveled with him to study in the scriptorium there.

The monks were sad because so many of their books had been destroyed or stolen by raiders. "They are sometimes sold on the Continent for a high price," they told Brian.

"If you know where they are, why don't you go and get them back?"

"Ah, Brian, life is not that easy!"

"Why not?" he wanted to know. But they could not tell him. No one could tell him why good people were slain, why treasures were stolen, why children had to grow up motherless. But he knew such things were wrong.

He knew they could be changed. Anything could be changed. Brian had seen change greater than he had ever imagined when Beal Boru was destroyed.

He felt something growing in him like a hard core. If no one else will make things right, I shall, he thought. He could not accept the world as it was.

Yet sometimes, alone in the night, he still felt like a small child, helpless and afraid. He did not tell anyone this. No one would care, he thought. Mahon had walked away and left him in the ruins of Beal Boru.

I have only myself, he thought. I must make that be enough.

But he had friends, too. Others wanted to be with him, because he was so good at everything he did. Brian was quick and clever and big for his age, and as the seasons passed he demanded more and more of himself. He had the woodcarver at the abbey make weapons for him out of wood, so he could practice with them since the monks forbade real ones. He worked just as hard at his lessons, and when his eyes burned and his head ached he did not let himself stop. I am studying how to win, he thought, reading of Charlemagne and Caesar.

When the wind howled up the Shannon, he missed Aval on her crag. Under the stern gaze of the monks he prayed to God and Christ and the gentle Virgin in chapel with the other students. But when he was alone, dreaming by the river at the end of day, he thought of the shee. He thought of an older Ireland and tried to imagine what it had been like before the foreigners came.

Brother Tomas understood. "Ancient Ireland? I shall teach you how to see it, Brian. Look in these books you study, with their illustrations. In their brilliant colors and free-flowing designs you can see our land as it was. You will see the land of saints and scholars, where an artist could paint with gold or make silver chalices and book boxes without having to fear they would be destroyed by heathen foreigners."

"Can Ireland be like that again?" Brian asked, his eyes glowing.

Brother Tomas shook his head sadly. "Ah, lad, times have changed. Times have changed."

But they can change again, thought Brian stubbornly.

From other students at Clonmacnois Brian heard a different version of history. Some of them belonged to Irish clans who had done their share of robbing monasteries, just like the Vikings, and boasted of what they had taken.

Brian was angry. "We can't be thieves and robbers just because the foreigners are. We have to be better than they are."

When Brian talked about being better, the other boys listened. They admired him because he really was the best of them, at both games and studies. They wanted to be like him, so they began following the lead he set.

The more Brian learned the more he wanted to know. He worked until he could play the harp as well as any harper, or recite the poems about ancient heroes as well as a bard. He even persuaded the carpenters and stonemasons who repaired the walls and buildings of Clonmacnois to teach him their skills.

"I want to know how to build the strongest, safest fortress in Ireland someday," he explained.

He was still very young, but when they looked into his eyes they did not laugh at him. They gave him tools and showed him how to use them, and he learned very fast.

Brian always seemed to be in a hurry. He had more energy than he could spend, and no day was long enough for all he wanted to do. But because he played as hard as he worked he was well loved at Clonmacnois. The monks soon learned they could usually find him at the center of a cluster of laughing friends.

They also learned, as his parents had known, that when there was mischief brewing Brian was usually to blame. Yet he would always admit it with a cheerful grin, and take his punishment without complaining. And he never did any real damage.

Brian had seen enough destruction at Beal Boru to last a lifetime.

But there was always news of more destruction and loss, it seemed. The fighting never stopped in Ireland. When Brian was beginning his second year of studies, word arrived that Kennedy of the Dalcassians, his father, had been killed in a battle against Callahan of the Owenacht clan, who was both King of Munster and a friend to the Danes of Limerick.

The abbot sent Brother Tomas to tell Brian. The monk found the boy where he often was in the late afternoons, on the footworn oval beyond the monastery where the students raced each other. Brian had just outrun a long-legged youth from Lough Ree and was grinning with victory, but his smile faded when he saw the expression on Brother Tomas's face.

He knew. Even before the monk opened his mouth, Brian knew something awful had happened. A great cold stone seemed to settle in the pit of his stomach.

"It's your father, I'm afraid," Brother Tomas said as gently as he could.

Brian tried to brace himself. "Is he ill? Injured?"

Instead of answering, the monk shook his head and dropped his eyes, unable to say the words.

Brian said them instead. "My father is dead."

"He is."

Dead, Brian thought. My father. While I have been running and laughing, my father has been lying dead.

He felt as if a half-forgotten nightmare had just come back to swallow him. He heard himself say, "How did it happen?"

Remembering that Brian was still a young boy,

Brother Tomas did not tell him many of the details. But Brian heard enough. When the monk finished by saying, "It is the will of God," the boy replied angrily, "It was the will of the man whose sword killed him!"

He would not forget Callahan of Munster, friend of the Danes. Friend of the Vikings and no better than they were.

I will be better than all of them, he promised himself. I will defeat every one of them and make them pay.

Then he whirled around and ran off before Brother Tomas could stop him. He ran to the edge of the river and crouched down among the reeds, so no one would see him cry.

Schooling ended in his sixteenth year, when a messenger sent by his brother Mahon arrived at Clonmacnois. "Brian mac Kennedy is old enough to take up weapons," the messenger said, "and is needed to fight with his tribe against its enemies."

The abbot protested. "The lad has a fine mind, too good to be split open with an ax." But in the end he had to let Brian go.

On the day before he was to leave, Brian suddenly felt unsure. Through all the years of his growing up he had dreamed of going to fight the foreigners. While other students looked first in one direction and then another, he had kept his eyes fixed on one goal. Since the day he sat on the ground beside his dead mother, he had been preparing himself to be a warrior and make certain such a thing could never happen to any other child.

It had been an exciting dream. But now the time had really come, and his mouth was dry with fear. I'm not ready, he thought. Let it happen tomorrow instead. I'm not ready yet!

In his dreams and plans he had always won, but Brian knew that the world beyond the walls of Clonmacnois was a dangerous place where dreams did not always come true. He was big for his age and strong, with a quick mind, but that might not be enough.

Beyond the walls death was waiting for him. He could smell it on the wind. He could almost hear the banshee cry.

More than anything else, he wanted to crawl into his bed and pull the covers over his head . . . and have Bebinn tuck him in.

But he was sixteen years old and childhood was over. There was no going back. He doubled his fists so no one would see that his hands were shaking, and went to say good-bye to his friends.

Mahon, who now led the Dalcassians, was camped near Killmallock. He had sent a small party of armed warriors to escort Brian to him, for no traveler was safe alone.

One of the escort was a man called Nessa, who was skilled in the use of the sling. ''Will you teach me to use the sling?'' Brian asked as they made their way south.

''The sling is not a noble weapon,'' Nessa told

him. "You will use a sword and spear."

"But I want to learn to use every sort of weapon, Nessa. A sword is no good at a distance."

"Spears are for distance."

"They are. But when you have thrown all your spears, what do you do then? With a sling, you can always pick up more stones and rearm yourself."

"Princes have never fought with slings," Nessa said firmly.

Brian scowled. " 'Never' is not a good enough reason."

The slinger gave him a surprised look. "Next you will be telling me you want to use an ax like the Vikings."

"I do want to learn to use the ax; it's a splendid weapon."

"The Gael do not use foreign axes!" Nessa was shocked.

"Then they should. Use the weapons the winners use. Doesn't that make sense?"

Before Nessa could think of an answer, they saw the leather tents of Mahon's camp in the distance. They were nearing Killmallock. Brian's heart began to pound. At last, he thought, his real life was about to begin. He felt a pang of fear and uncertainty, but before it could weaken him he made himself run forward eagerly, calling Mahon's name. Nessa had to hurry after him to tell the sentries to let him through.

Once Brian joined Mahon's army of Dalcassians, there was no more time for doubts. Learning

to be a warrior was very hard work and kept him busy from sunrise to sunset. The other warriors were not gentle with him. He was Mahon's brother, but he must prove his own manhood. They laughed at his lack of a beard. They made fun of the softness of his hands. When one of them caught him alone, they beat him.

Brian did not complain to his brother. He had learned the hard lesson that pain is endured alone. He simply worked harder to be stronger and better at fighting. Then, one by one, he attacked the men who had bullied him and beat them badly.

In time even the grizzled old warriors who had fought with Kennedy were watching him with a respectful light in their eyes. "The young Lion of Thomond," they called him behind his back.

"He has no fear in him," they said.

When he learned of this he whispered the name to himself in the night, as he lay rolled in his cloak, sleeping on the ground among the other warriors. "Lion of Thomond." Brian's lips shaped the words proudly. They made him forget his aches and bruises.

He had learned to act brave no matter how he felt inside. As time passed, he began to believe it himself. If you ran forward eagerly and shouted and yelled when you were afraid, the fear went away . . . most of the time.

In the Year of Our Lord 955, Donal, son of Murtach, had become High King of Ireland, the *Árd Rí*, king of the provincial kings. Donal was not fond of fighting. He found it easier to let the foreigners have their way, and so local chieftains were left to defend themselves.

Mahon struggled to protect the land of Thomond from the Danes of Limerick, but it was not easy. The river was under the control of the Vikings for most of its length, and the longships pillaged almost at will. In addition, the Irish west of the Shannon had to pay crushing taxes.

Resisting the Vikings was expensive. Men must be supplied with weapons and food, and the Vikings were impoverishing the countryside. In desperation, Mahon at last plundered Clonmacnois for Church treasures that could be sold to pay for swords and spears and horses.

Brian was so angry over this that the two brothers had a terrible argument. "No matter what happens, we must not steal from our own people!" Brian yelled at Mahon in the command tent.

Mahon sighed wearily. The years of war were showing on him. He was still a young man but he looked old. His broad shoulders had begun to droop and there was a frost of white in his coppery hair. "You don't understand, Brian. This is war, us against them. We have to use every resource."

"And that means robbing the monasteries?"

"If we must."

"No!" Brian shouted, slamming his fist against his open palm.

This was one of many arguments between the two. Brian had studied the campaigns of the great military leaders of the past, and when he compared these to the way Mahon and the Dalcassians waged war he thought he saw many mistakes. He could not resist pointing these out to his brother, who did not thank him for it.

"It was a mistake to educate you," Mahon growled. "Now you think you know more than anyone else."

"I don't think that. But I do know that history is full of valuable lessons and we don't seem to be learning them."

"History is ashes," said Mahon scornfully. "I understand the situation today. I know how to fight here and now."

"If you did," Brian pointed out, "you would be winning. But you're not winning. The Danes are stronger than ever. They take the cattle from our fields, they burn our homesteads for pleasure, they do to others what they did to us at Beal Boru, and you aren't stopping them."

Mahon's face turned red. "Get out of my tent."

Someday Brian would look back on these as the skirmish years, years of running, bent over, through the heather, either to or from a battle that was rarely won. The Dalcassians grew thin and hard but the Danes were harder, and their axes sang. Step by step, Mahon surrendered the land of Thomond his ancestors had won on the battlefield.

Deep in his heart Mahon began to think Callahan and Donal were right. It was impossible to defeat the Vikings. Let them take what they wanted. Perhaps it would be better to accept it, to bow the head and look away when the Dane passed by, in the hope that he would leave you in peace.

Mahon was growing weary.

But Brian was not tired. Though they were not welcome, he kept bringing his brother new schemes for overcoming the enemy. "If we had men on horseback, like the cavalry the Romans used under Caesar, we could move faster and surround the Viking line," he suggested.

"Only princes ride horses and it's hard enough to get horses for them," Mahon replied. "This is another of your wild ideas, Brian. Who ever heard of common warriors on horseback?"

"I just told you. Caesar—"

"Forget about Caesar!" Mahon said angrily. "We don't fight that way. Those are a child's fancies."

Brian's eyes grew hard. "I'm not a child anymore."

"Then stop thinking like one."

Brian could not stop thinking, however. Though he knew his brother would not listen, he could not help suggesting another idea. "The Vikings use the rivers as roads. Why don't we build boats of our own and fill them with warriors? Then we could meet the enemy on the water and turn them back before they can do any damage to people in the settlements along the river."

"We aren't sailors, Brian, we are cattle lords. We know the land, not the water."

"We could learn."

Mahon looked at his brother. Now almost seventeen years old, Brian had become the tallest of the Dalcassians, a head taller than Mahon himself. He was lean and rawboned, with a strong nose and a face as freckled as a blackbird's egg. His hair was long and wild and he combed it only before going into battle.

"Who would teach our men to handle boats, Brian?" Mahon asked him. "Who has time?"

"I could."

"You've never even been in a boat."

"I could learn, and teach others. I know how to learn, Mahon."

"Are you saying I don't?"

"I'm saying you won't, and that's a mistake. If you would let me lead just a few men, we could capture one boat and I could take it apart and put it back together to see how it was made. Then we could build our own."

Mahon rubbed his hand across his tired eyes. "You're howling into the wind, Brian. You're wasting my time with this foolishness." His voice was angry.

The two glared at each other. Without thinking, Brian knotted his fists as he did when he was about to fight. When he realized what he was doing he opened his hands. "We are about to become enemies," he said to Mahon. "What's happening to us?"

"You're trying to tell me how to lead my army

and I won't allow it! I was named King of Thomond on the sacred mound of Magh Adhair where Dalcassian kings have always been inaugurated. My words command the tribe. You will not argue with me."

Brian knotted his fists again. "I shall when you're wrong!"

The air between them became white with anger.

The final break came because of Callahan, king of the province of Munster. It was learned that Callahan was not only trading openly with the Danes, but was also letting them take young Irish boys and girls as slaves. When some Dalcassian children were seized in a raid, Brian's temper exploded.

"The King of Munster is betraying his own people to the Vikings!" he roared at Mahon. "What are you going to do about it?"

"What do you expect me to do, march on Cashel?"

"I do expect it! March on his stronghold at Cashel and overthrow the traitor. Rule Munster in his place. Our grandfather Lorcan once claimed to be King of Munster; you have the right."

Mahon looked doubtful. "That may just have been the boasting of the poets, Brian."

"Then make it come true. End the Owenacht control of the south. Many will support you. I've been talking to the warriors here and many agree with me."

"Others will not. Tribes who have shared in Danish plunder would turn against me, Brian. I would be making more enemies for us if I rose against Callahan. My duty is to defend Thomond, not to try to seize control of all Munster.''

"But don't you see? You can't defend Thomond unless you do control Munster. The king of the province is supposed to defend the small tribal kingdoms, that's why we pay him taxes. But Callahan isn't defending us. We have only ourselves, and that isn't good enough. Challenge him.''

"If my army can't defeat a Danish raiding party, how do you expect it to defeat the army of Callahan and seize the Rock of Cashel? You're dreaming, Brian.''

The young man nodded. "I am a dreamer," he admitted. "But every great deed begins with a dream. You would be surprised how many men in this camp share this one with me.''

"So that's it," Mahon said bitterly. "This isn't about me challenging Callahan. This is really about you challenging me for the leadership of the Dalcassians. I see it now. You've been winning my men away from me behind my back. It is you who is the traitor, Brian. Get out of my sight, get out of my camp!'' Mahon shouted.

Brian stared at him in horror. He had only been trying to help. He could hardly believe Mahon had misunderstood so completely. But he was too proud to argue any further.

I have lost him, Brian thought to himself, as I have lost my mother and my father. The pain stabbed very deeply. But he drew himself up to his full height and said only, ''If that's what you want, Mahon.''

Then he turned and walked away.

FOUR

The Rebels

When Brian left Mahon's camp, he did not leave alone. A number of warriors, particularly the younger ones, were willing to follow wherever he might lead.

He did not ask them to come with him. He reminded them, "You are sworn to my brother, the leader of the Dalcassians."

But they said, "Your words do you honor, and that makes us all the more eager to be with you. You're a better warrior than Mahon. We win when we follow you. When we keep our eyes on his standard, we find ourselves losing too often."

Brian was pleased at these words, but he could not let them see it. He knew it was wrong to draw warriors away from the king of the tribe, but he also knew Mahon was not leading the men in the direction they wanted to go . . . to victory.

"If you are determined," he told them, "come with me, and I promise we shall do our best to defeat the Vikings."

Mahon stood in front of his tent, with his arms folded, and watched his younger brother ride away, followed by almost sixty warriors on foot. Their spears gleamed in the sunlight.

Once they were out of sight of Killmallock, Brian made himself put Mahon out of his mind. It was not easy. He knew he was now a leader of men who would expect much of him and judge him harshly if he failed. He also knew he was very young; almost all of them were older. Yet they expected him to show them the way and tell them what to do.

He rode for a time without saying anything. Then suddenly he reined in his horse and slid to the ground. Tossing the reins to one of the spear carriers, he told the men, "I'll walk with you. We're in this together."

They were surprised. Leaders always set themselves apart. But Brian was different.

He led them to the hills beyond the Shannon, where he knew every cave and glen and possible hiding place. There they set up a series of camps, so they could move swiftly from place to place. Brian wanted to be ready to fight the Vikings wherever he met them.

After a rainstorm, he found a Viking battle ax

half-buried in mud. When he picked it up he saw the fearful way his men looked at the weapon. He set himself the task of learning how to use it with either hand, practicing alone until he was as skillful as a Dane. Then he began searching for other axes that might have been lost in the many battles in Thomond. When he had enough, he taught his men to use them.

The next time his warriors met a Viking raiding party, the Irish attacked the Danes with their own weapons. The startled Vikings were terrified. They had never had to face the axes before. They fled, howling.

That night Brian's men cheered him in the Thomond hills.

"The axes did not win the battle," he told them. "We won because we surprised the enemy. We shall surprise them again."

And so they did.

In his camp at Killmallock, Mahon began hearing of his younger brother's successes against the Danes. "It is not good having this split in the Dalcassians," Mahon told his captains.

"We need Brian here," the captains replied. "He and his men should be fighting with us, not off on their own somewhere. It's your fault, Mahon, that we have lost such good warriors."

Mahon sent messengers into the Clare hills northwest of the Shannon, which was the part of Thomond to which Brian had taken his men. "Tell him I order him to return to my camp at Killmallock, and we shall forget the quarrel between us,'' Mahon told the messengers.

But they returned to him without Brian. ''We could not find him or his men anywhere,'' they reported.

''Are they not there?''

''They are there. But they only come out of their hiding places to kill Vikings. Otherwise your brother stays so well hidden no one can find him, and the people whose homes he is protecting will tell no one where he is. They don't want to lose him.''

Mahon scowled, wishing he could claim such loyalty.

Brian's outlaw band in the hills was, however, growing smaller as men were killed in battles with the Danes of Limerick. Brian knew he could not get any more men from his brother. But the tribe whose territory lay just north of Dalcassian land, on the Galway border, had plenty of strong young fighting men. Brian decided to visit them and see if he could persuade some of their warriors to join him.

The slinger called Nessa, who had left Mahon to follow Brian, warned him with a laugh, ''I hear that the king of that tribe has a number of daughters he wants to marry to princes of other tribes, Brian. Be careful, or you will come back with a woman riding behind you on your horse.''

Brian laughed, too. ''A woman's arms around my waist would slow me down too much, Nessa. I don't need a wife,'' he said.

Taking a score of well-armed warriors with him, he rode to meet the king called Edigan. Edigan lived in a ring fort very like Beal Boru, but instead of many sons, he did, indeed, have many daughters. He was eager to have Brian take one of his daughters in marriage.

"She would have to be willing to marry you, of course," Edigan said. "We observe the old Irish law, the Brehon law, and that says no woman can be married without her consent."

"The Dalcassians observe the same law," Brian replied. "But I have not said I am willing to marry."

Edigan smiled and stroked his big red beard. "Let me send for my daughters. At least see them."

One by one, the young women entered the lodge. Some were thin and some were sallow, but one was beautiful. She had dark curls and the sweetest face Brian had ever seen. He could not take his eyes off her.

Edigan smiled again. "You are seventeen, Brian mac Kennedy," he said. "It is time for you to be married. Give me a bride-gift of twelve cows for that girl and she is yours. We will then be related by marriage and I shall allow warriors of my tribe to join your band of fighting men and protect your homeland from the raiders."

Brian was building a name for himself as the bravest of men. But his courage deserted him when he tried to ask the dark-haired girl to marry him. He could hardly even say her name, which was Mor. His tongue stumbled over the word and he felt his cheeks burn.

Mor was blushing, too, but there was also laughter in her eyes. She knew from the first moment she saw Brian that she wanted to be his wife. His shyness delighted her. He was so very tall, and so very muscular, she had not expected he would be gentle as well. Yet when he took her hand in his and asked her to marry him, he held her fingers as if they would break, and she knew he would never hurt her.

I will be safe with this man, she thought. "I shall marry you, Brian mac Kennedy," she agreed.

Brian felt as if the sun had just come up.

He did not even hear the way his men teased him. "Nessa was right," they said, "and our brave leader has fallen into the oldest trap of all."

Brian only smiled dreamily. "She has blue eyes," he said. "Did you ever see such blue eyes?"

He returned to Thomond with a score of Edigan's kinsmen to add to his band of warriors. At once he sent word to his brother Marcan, who was now a priest, telling him that he was to be married and asking Marcan to say the Christian words at the ceremony.

Brian also sent a message to Mahon, inviting him to come to the wedding, which would be held at a small stone church north of Beal Boru. Brian instructed the messenger, "Tell my brother to bring only a small party of my closest kinsmen with him. He must leave his warriors on duty, guarding Thomond more keenly than ever, while he is away from them. Tell him to be certain he has plenty of men posted along every road and path the Limerick Danes use into our land. And sentries on the high ground along the river," Brian added.

When Mahon received this message, he had mixed feelings. Brian had invited him to the wedding, which meant the quarrel between them was set aside. But Brian was still trying to tell his older brother how to order his army!

"The Vikings are quiet at this time of year," Mahon told his captains, "and there is no need for every man we have to be on guard. I want them with me, to remind my brother and his followers how powerful the King of Thomond is."

So a huge party was gathered. The Dalcassians all wanted to attend Brian's wedding. Not only were his deeds making him famous, but also everyone knew that if anything happened to Mahon, Brian himself would become King of Thomond, Chieftain of the Dalcassians. So it was important to be seen at his wedding.

When Brian saw the crowds arriving he knew Mahon had ignored his words. The king had brought his army with him to the wedding.

Brian bit his lip and did not say anything about it to his brother. He was very glad to see Mahon. Perhaps it would be all right. He did not want to start another argument, so he hugged Mahon and bade him welcome.

Mahon was relieved. Perhaps I will be able to take him and his warriors back to Killmallock when the wedding is over, he thought to himself, after the honeymoon—the month-long period when Brian will want to be alone with his new wife and the two of them drink honey mead together.

"How did you win such a beautiful girl?" Mahon asked his younger brother.

Brian shook his head. "I truly don't know. Perhaps it was when I played my harp for her."

Mahon grinned. "You are a harper as well as a warrior. A man of many talents. No wonder we keep hearing stories about you and your deeds. They're calling you the Lion of Thomond."

Brian dropped his eyes. How good it felt to have his brother with him again, and to hear such words from Mahon.

The sun shone, the day was beautiful. Marcan married Brian and Mor in the sight of God, and then the singing and dancing and feasting began. It should have been the happiest day of Brian's life. And yet . . . from time to time he found himself looking toward the skyline as if he expected to see Vikings in the distance, waving axes . . .

FIVE

Mahon, King of Munster

It did not take the Danes of Limerick long to learn that Thomond was unprotected. Even as Brian and the Dalcassians were celebrating the wedding, Viking raiders fanned out across the countryside. They looted and burned; they slaughtered Irish cattle in the field and took the best parts away with them, leaving the carcasses to rot.

A terrified farmer came to tell Mahon what was happening. "Where are your warriors to protect us?" the man cried.

Brian was very angry. "I warned you!" he shouted at Mahon. "Didn't I send word to you to leave Thomond well guarded along its borders?"

Mahon drew himself up stiffly. "I don't take orders from you."

"You would not take my advice simply because it came from *me*," Brian charged. "You never listen to me because you're jealous of your authority. Now you see what it has cost!"

Mahon knew Brian's words were true. He could never admit the younger man was right. He was the king.

They glared at each other with all the old anger rising between them.

"I think you had better leave now," Brian said coldly. "Go back to Killmallock. Go try to explain to the people whose homes are destroyed for the sake of your pride."

"I was hoping you would come with me," Mahon started to say. Then his anger overcame him. He would not ask Brian for anything. He turned away and began gathering his men.

When Brian saw them marching away he wanted to run after them. But he did not. He was as proud as Mahon.

He took his new wife to Beal Boru, where she would live in the rebuilt lodge that had belonged to his parents. Brian himself spent most of his time in the nearby hills and valleys, protecting the area. It was doubly precious to him now.

The Vikings controlled the river, but Brian held the highlands. At night, in camp, he studied by fire-light the books he kept with him, books describing the successful wars of Alexander and Charlemagne. Books telling how to win.

He learned new ways of outwitting the enemy.

He learned how to take advantage of mist and fog to make a few men seem like a larger number. They shouted until their voices echoed throughout the hills, like the cries of an army.

From his books Brian also learned new battle formations. Using a stick to draw in the dirt, he showed his warriors ways of fighting they had never seen before. Until now, Irish men had just run at each other in a broad line. But Brian showed them how to break up that line into wings and flanks and circles, and how to get behind the enemy and surround him.

They won more victories. The Vikings learned to be afraid of Brian. They were the first to call him Brian Boru, after the place he fought to protect.

Between battles, Brian sometimes climbed alone to the heights where the gray crag jutted out against the sky. He gazed down at the great blue lake called Lough Derg, and the rebuilt fort where Mor was awaiting the birth of their first child.

He could sense the guardian spirit of his tribe close beside him. "Watch over my family, Aval," he whispered to the banshee, knowing she could hear him.

In southern Thomond, Mahon heard reports. Brian's band fought brilliantly, but they were heavily outnumbered. Slowly, man by man, the Vikings were killing them. There were so few rebels with Brian in the hills, and so many Vikings.

Almost as if he meant to insult Mahon, the Viking King of Limerick was concentrating on Brian

Boru and all but ignoring the King of the Dalcassians. Ivar the Dane, King of Limerick, considered Brian more dangerous than his brother and wanted to see him dead.

Mor worried about her husband. Brian came to see her as often as he could, but they never had much time together. She would hear his familiar whistle ringing from the hills, and when she ran to the gate to meet him he would take her in his arms and swing her around and around, laughing. But he always left at first light, going back to his warriors.

Brian hated to leave. The lodge was warm and snug, with fresh reeds on the floor and brightly colored woolen rugs hanging on the walls to keep out drafts. Mor wove those rugs on her loom, and kept his harp safe for him when he was in the hills. Puppies, descended from his father's hounds, slept beside the central firepit, and on baking days the whole fort smelled of the bread Mor baked in the beehive-shaped stone oven.

Beal Boru was home again, the home Brian thought he had lost. But in order to keep it safe he could not stay to enjoy it.

The year of Brian's marriage had been a year of important deaths in Munster. First the chief poet of the province died. Soon after came the death of the Tanist, who stood second in line for the kingship of Munster.

The next spring Brian's first son, Murcha, was born. At almost the same time the King of Munster died, leaving the kingship vacant. The province was ruled from the royal stronghold at Cashel, which was thrown into confusion by the king's death.

Mahon was not surprised when Brian came down out of the hills and confronted him in his camp. "Claim the kingship," he said bluntly.

Mahon looked at his brother. Fighting hard and living rough had made the boy a mighty man. He was the tallest of all the Dalcassians, with eyes as gray as winter skies over Lough Derg, and a jaw as firm as the stones of Slieve Bernagh. By now only a few of his followers were still alive, but he stood as if there were an army at his back. "Claim the kingship," he demanded again. "My warriors and I will support you."

Mahon could have laughed at the idea of that battered band being any help to him in claiming Cashel. "It would take more help than you could give me," he told Brian. "The Owenacht tribe are very powerful in Munster and would oppose me. They have a strong claim to the kingship."

"Our grandfather Lorcan was called the King of Munster," Brian reminded him. "It is time we made that boast a truth."

He looked totally confident. Mahon could hardly believe his eyes. Brian was lean and ragged and battle-scarred, but still managed to look as if he could never lose. How does he do it? Mahon wondered.

Brian wore his courage like armor, and kept his secret fears to himself. "I heard a rumor that you made peace with the Danes of Limerick,'' he said suddenly.

Mahon was startled. ''How did you . . . Who told you that?''

''It doesn't matter. Is it true? I did not want to believe it until I heard it from your own lips.''

Mahon hesitated, but he could not hide the truth from Brian's sharp eyes. ''I have made peace with the Danes,'' he admitted at last. ''My warriors were exhausted, and harvest season had come. They needed to be able to care for their farms and families.''

Brian understood. But he said, ''You made a great mistake, brother. Never trust the foreigners. We can use your mistake, however. There is always a way to profit from an error if you give it some thought, and I've been thinking about this one.

''While Ivar of Limerick thinks you are willing to stop fighting him, he may be willing to let you become King of Munster without opposing you. He knows you, remember. He does not know whatever man the Owenachts may wish to make king.''

''Are you suggesting I ask for the support of the Vikings?'' asked Mahon, astonished to hear this from Brian.

Brian smiled a faint, wry smile. ''I am not. I'm just telling you to take advantage of what you have. Proclaim yourself King of Munster now, take everyone by surprise, and my men and I will help you take Cashel.''

Mahon was tempted. The Dalcassians and the Owenachts were ancient enemies, and an Owenacht had killed Kennedy in a battle between the two tribes. It would be very satisfying to deny the Owenachts the kingship of Munster. "But what about afterward?" he asked Brian. "If I do become king of the province, what will you do?"

A faraway look came into the younger man's eyes. "I'll go home to my wife and son, and eat fish fresh-caught from the weir on the Shannon below Beal Boru."

"But wouldn't you want to bring your family to live at Cashel?"

Brian raised one eyebrow. "You may have made peace with the Danes, but I haven't. You rule Munster. I'll continue to protect that part of Munster that is Thomond. Cashel is not my home."

And so, in the Year of Our Lord 959, Mahon mac Kennedy claimed the title of King of Munster and captured the stone fortress atop the Rock of Cashel. Because the time had been shrewdly chosen, he was not challenged. Surprised by his swift and unexpected move, the Owenacht chieftains did not have a prince ready to stand against him. Besides, they were uncertain about risking the anger of the Danes of Limerick, who seemed willing to let Mahon be king. So they accepted the situation, for a time. But their resentment simmered like a pot coming to the boil.

Brian saw his brother crowned King of Munster, then true to his word, he returned to Beal Boru. As he had known they would, the Danes continued raiding in Thomond, no matter what truce Ivar had made with Mahon. Thomond was too rich a land to be spared by the Vikings.

While the new King of Munster ate fat meat in his stronghold on the Rock of Cashel, Brian went back to sleeping wrapped in his cloak, through wind and rain, in the hills of Clare, and protecting his homeland.

He had quietly recruited a number of new followers from among Mahon's own warriors, while Mahon was being crowned king. Brian believed in taking advantage of opportunities.

But once more his numbers were reduced through almost constant fighting until word reached the King of Munster that Brian was almost the lone survivor. This time Mahon went to him. He found him wrapped in wolfskins, camping in a limestone cave.

"Look at you," said Mahon. "Bashed and bloody and weary. You with two babies and another on the way, I hear. Give up now, Brian. Come to the south, come to Cashel and live with us. We shall make your family very welcome."

Brian's gray eyes met his with a steady gaze. "I won't abandon Thomond to the Vikings. Neither our father nor our grandfather surrendered this land, and I will not."

"But don't you see, Brian, that it's impossible to defeat the foreigners? There are so many of them— the Danes in Limerick and Waterford, the Norsemen in Dublin—they're everywhere now. They have terrible weapons and coats of mail. If you keep on fighting you'll surely be killed one day.''

Brian gazed sadly at the brother he had once admired so much. "It's natural for men to die," he said, "and death in battle is better than a life in slavery to foreigners.

"But one thing is not natural, not for Dalcassians. We have never submitted to outrage or insult. You shame us, asking that we do so now. We would be forever dishonored if we gave up the land for which our ancestors died.

"And we don't have to, Mahon! The Danes can be beaten. I myself have beaten them many times with a much smaller force of men. Once I cleared the countryside of them from Lough Derg all the way to the river Fergus, with only a handful of warriors beside me. While you, with your much larger army, did nothing to help," he added bitterly.

Mahon cleared his throat. "What if I had helped you and been willing to fight your way?"

"By now the strength of the Danes would be broken in Munster," Brian told him.

"If that is true," said Mahon, "I regret that I didn't listen."

My brother is the man I thought he was! Brian thought joyously. Aloud he said, "Regret is a waste of time. We have today. And tomorrow."

"You would still fight for me?"

"You are the King of Munster," Brian replied. "If you will declare war on the Danes again I will fight at your shoulder until we drive them from our land forever.''

Staring at his brother, Mahon knew those words were true. Brian would fight alone or with an army, but he would fight. Nothing could stop him.

SIX

Boru!

The King of Munster summoned the heads of the Dalcassian families to a council. Each clan leader arrived in full battle dress, with a shortsword in a leather scabbard at his hip, and a train of attendants following him up the steep pathway to the top of the Rock of Cashel.

When they were gathered in the great feasting hall, Mahon spoke to them. He used many of the words Brian had used. "If we do not make a stand and fight the Danes of Limerick now it will be too late," he told the Dalcassians. "They have their hands around our throats. I have said nothing, for the sake of peace, but the time has come to throw off the clutching hand."

Many of the clan leaders were men who, like

Mahon, had lost heart over the years and been willing to settle for submission to the power of the Vikings. But when they heard the King of Munster speaking in this way, they became excited. They put their hands on their sword hilts and their eyes shone.

"Throw off the clutching hand of the Vikings," they said to one another, nodding agreement.

Some of them noticed the tall, silent young warrior who stood in the shadows, watching them with measuring eyes.

"That is Brian, the one they call the Lion of Thomond," the whisper went around the room.

A vote was taken. The decision was war.

An army camp was set up around the base of the Rock of Cashel, and warriors were summoned from every tribe that had a duty to supply the king with fighting men. Soon the Dalcassians were joined by warriors from many other southern tribes.

Ivar, the Danish king of Limerick, was very angry when he learned of this. "Mahon betrays the peace he made with me!" he cried in his huge boat-shaped hall beside the Shannon. He summoned all the Danes of Munster, as well as the Irish who were connected to them through trade or marriage. He demanded the loyalty of these Irish in the war to come. When some of them refused, he had them put to death to serve as a lesson to the rest.

The Danish army marched from Limerick toward Cashel. The Irish forces broke camp and set out to meet them. But the Irish leaders were not in agreement about the way to fight the Vikings. Brian had been explaining his ideas about battle formations to the older chieftains, and they complained to Mahon. "Your brother has strange ideas," they said. "He wants us to fight in ways we have never fought before. Each of us is used to leading his own men in his own way. We want no part of this new plan."

Mahon tried to keep peace between Brian and the chieftains.

"You must not insist on your own ideas," he told his brother.

"They are not my ideas. They are battle plans that have worked for the most famous military leaders in history. If we were to use flankers, instead of meeting the Danes in one single broad line . . ."

"I don't want to hear this again," Mahon said wearily.

It was hard for Brian to plead, but he made himself say, "Please, Mahon. You are the king. If you give the order they will follow it. Order them to take the positions I suggest when they face the Danes."

Mahon locked eyes with his younger brother. A struggle of wills heated the air between them until Brian thought it would burst into flame, but he never blinked. Finally Mahon was the one to drop his eyes. "I shall do as you ask," he said. "But I warn you, Brian. Though the men may take up the positions, they won't fight from them. Once they see the enemy they will each fight in the old way; they will never follow you."

The army of Mahon met the army of Ivar at dawn, at a place called Sulcoit. Much of the land was covered with trees, making fighting difficult. The Danes advanced at sunrise across one of the few stretches of open meadowland, holding up their axes as they came, to frighten the Irish with them.

But Brian's Dalcassians had axes, too, and he had taught them how to use them.

In spite of this, Mahon's warriors stared fearfully at the Danes. They had not expected such an enormous number. The Irish who had joined with Ivar made his army very large indeed. Mahon's men, in the battle formation Brian had planned, could not make themselves move forward. They could only stand and watch the sea of death flooding toward them across the meadowland.

Then one man started forward. All alone. To meet the enemy.

Fear filled Brian's belly like a great, cold stone, but he did not let the fear show on his face. Mahon's army was frightened enough. They must see someone who did not appear to be afraid.

He marched forward alone, with his sword in his hand, as if Ivar and the Danes meant nothing to him. He left his horse behind, choosing to fight on foot like a common warrior. Only Mahon and the tribal leaders were mounted, sitting on their horses and staring at Brian as he did this mad, reckless, incredibly brave thing.

Cold sweat ran down Brian's back. He lifted his sword higher, so it caught the light of the rising sun. He walked on, waiting for the first Danish spear to hiss through the air and strike him down.

That would at least make Mahon's army angry enough to throw off its fear and to attack, Brian thought. He did not want to die. But he was more afraid of losing.

No spear was hurled from Ivar's side. His warriors were all staring at Brian, too. Vikings admired courage above all else, and the red-haired young giant approaching them filled them with awe. They knew they would never again see anything like this, one man in splendid defiance against thousands.

To Brian it seemed as if everything happened very, very slowly, as if there were all the time in the world that morning. He walked on and on, expecting to die. Two armies seemed frozen, watching him. And then at last he heard behind him the first stirrings of Mahon's army shaking off its fear and beginning to move.

Someone shouted Brian's name. Another voice took it up and the cry swept through the Irish ranks. "Brian Boru!" they chanted as they started forward, drawn by his courage.

"Brian Boru, Boru, Boru!" They chanted in rhythm as they broke into a run, holding the pattern he had set for them.

Swords lifted. Slings whirled in the air. Spears clashed against shields making an awful din. Mahon's army thundered across the meadowland toward the enemy, shouting a new battle cry. A cry both terrible and glorious.

"Boru! BORU! *BORU!*"

No longer alone, Brian was now running, too, leading the Munstermen. His fear was gone. His heart was singing inside him. He felt as if he could fly, as if no weapon could ever kill him.

The two armies came together with a crash of iron and the screams from thousands of throats.

On that summer morning at Sulcoit in the Year of Our Lord 968, the warriors of Munster gave Ivar's forces the worst defeat they had ever known.

By midday the Danes and their allies had given up the battle and were running for their lives. Some sought safety in the forest, some hid in the hedges. Others fled to Ivar's stronghold at Limerick, twenty miles away.

Mahon intended to stop and celebrate victory, but Brian said "Julius Caesar won great victories for Rome because he followed a beaten enemy and destroyed them totally, so he didn't have to fight them again a fortnight later."

Mahon was willing to listen to Brian now. The chieftains of Munster were all willing to listen to Brian now.

They set off in pursuit of the enemy, chanting "Boru!"

Brian and Mahon captured Limerick, where they

found and freed hundreds of Irish children the Danes had taken as slaves. In .Ivar's storehouses they found the loot of Munster: beautifully crafted Irish jewelry and ornaments of gold and silver and bronze, bales of wool and linen, stacks of leather, tools and weapons and harnesses, cups and goblets and chalices and book boxes decorated with gold and silver and precious stones.

Looking at the wealth stolen from his people, Brian thought of his mother lying murdered in the ashes of Beal Boru. She had died so a Viking could add her trinkets to his piles of plunder.

Without asking permission of Mahon, Brian ordered the warriors to plunder and burn Limerick. Then he took the prisoners of war to a hill called Singland and there executed every man who was fit for battle, whether they were Danes or Irishmen who had fought with the Danes.

Much, much later he would admit to his brother Marcan, "I had my revenge, but when the killing was over and the fires of Limerick died I felt empty inside. Why is that?"

Marcan said, "Because revenge does not bring back the dead, Brian. It only creates more dead."

After their defeat, Ivar and his surviving followers managed to get to Scattery Island in the Shannon and build a fort for themselves there. In time, they began raiding again. The Munstermen fought back, following Brian's battle plans. Even the most stubborn old chieftain admitted, "Brian Boru knows how to win."

Brian did know how to win. After seven defeats, Ivar the Dane fled for a time to safety in Wales. He was no longer willing to challenge the Lion of Thomond.

For six years, Mahon ruled Munster in peace, and was given tribute and warriors by the kings of the Munster tribes. But one called Molloy of Desmond, who was an Owenacht, complained that he should be King of Munster instead of Mahon. He and his friend, Donovan of Bruree, had enjoyed profitable trade with Ivar and his Danes and blamed Mahon for their loss of wealth.

Molloy and Donovan began to plot together against Mahon. They called on him at Cashel and urged him to show Christian forgiveness to Ivar, so the Dane could return to Limerick.

"Ivar is a changed man, and will make no more trouble," they claimed.

"Don't listen to them," Brian urged Mahon. "Molloy wants Ivar back to be his ally and help him take the kingship of Munster from you. And Ivar would surely do it to have revenge against you."

"You are too quick to believe the worst of others," said Mahon. "We have won peace, Brian. Accept it and enjoy it. I believe Molloy and Donovan, they have sworn loyalty to me, and I ask you to trust my judgment in this. Remember," he added with a frown, "I *am* the king."

Brian bit his lip and did not answer.

Since he had been with Mahon at Cashel, he had developed a curious habit. Every night before he went to sleep, Brian climbed to the top of the stone wall surrounding the king's stronghold. From there he could look across the fertile plains of Munster to the distant mountains.

He liked to think he could smell the breeze blowing off the Shannon. He pretended that the scent of flowers in the air was really the perfume from the hair of Aval on her gray crag.

Brian was lonely. At Mahon's urging, he had brought his family to Cashel, and Mor had sickened and died there during one of his campaigns against the Vikings. She left behind her four small children, and new shadows in Brian's eyes. Alone in the night, when no one could see, sometimes he wept for his dead wife.

And sometimes, when the wind sang to him, he thought Aval was calling him home to Beal Boru.

Brian was teaching his oldest son, Murcha, to ride a horse when word reached Cashel of a meeting of chieftains at Donovan's stronghold near Bruree. The King of Munster was invited.

Leaving Murcha, Brian ran to the great hall. Bursting in upon Mahon he cried, "Don't go!"

The king bristled. "Who are you to tell me what I can and cannot do?"

"I am your brother who wants to keep you safe, and I tell you, you must not go to this meeting. I do not trust the people involved."

"I shall request a promise of safety from the

Bishop of Cork himself," Mahon said. "Will that satisfy you?"

"Nothing would satisfy me but going with you to protect you."

"That I won't do, Brian. You are too hot-blooded; you might say or do something that would cause trouble."

"The trouble is already there, waiting for you!"

But Mahon would not listen. "You may understand warfare, Brian," he said. "But I understand kingship. This is a meeting of the leaders of Munster and I must go."

He left wearing a woolen cloak striped in the six colors of kingship, and carrying on his breast a sacred reliquary that was supposed to hold a fragment of the writings of St. Finnbarr. "This holy object will keep me safe," he assured Brian.

"Only a sword, my sword, would keep you safe," Brian muttered. He watched from the walls as Mahon rode away.

SEVEN

Brian, King of Munster

A messenger sent by the Bishop of Cork brought the news: "Mahon mac Kennedy was taken prisoner by Donovan of Bruree. Donovan surrendered him to Molloy of Desmond, who claims to be the rightful King of Munster. Mahon was sent to Molloy's stronghold with an escort of priests. On the way, Molloy's men attacked them and killed Mahon. The priests with him were, of course, unarmed, and could not protect him. As he was dying, the king flung the holy relic of St. Finnbarr into the bushes to keep from staining it with his blood."

Brian let out a cry of grief and rage. This latest loss was too much to bear. It was made worse, if that were possible, by the fact that Molloy and Donovan were Irish and not Vikings.

"Our own people," Brian said through gritted teeth, "killing their king. I'll make them pay."

"I thought you told me vengeance didn't satisfy you," said Marcan the priest.

"Did I? Then I was wrong. I'm going to take great satisfaction from hunting down Mahon's killers and killing them!"

Leaving his children, Murcha, Sive, Conor, and Flan, in safekeeping at Cashel, Brian went north to the sacred mound of Magh Adhair. There he was inaugurated as Prince of Thomond, the title formerly held by Mahon. Now the Dalcassians were officially his to command, following his banner of the three red lions.

Brian had many cousins who might have tried to claim the title of Prince of Thomond, but none dared oppose him.

At the head of the Dalcassian warriors, Brian planned an attack on Ivar the Dane. "When that man returned from Wales my brother should have killed him at once, instead of allowing him to settle on Scattery Island again," Brian told his followers. "Ivar is our enemy, and I suspect he played some part in the murder of Mahon. When he is dead, Molloy and Donovan will have lost a powerful ally."

Brian assembled a small fleet of boats in the Shannon as he had always wanted to do. With his Dalcassians manning this seedling navy, he attacked Ivar in his stronghold on Scattery Island. At the end of the day the place was in flames and its

inhabitants, including Ivar, were slain.

Next Brian went after Donovan. He found him at Bruree. Also in hiding there was Harald, a son of Ivar of Limerick. This was proof of Brian's suspicions—the Danes had been heavily involved in the plotting between Molloy and Donovan. Brian executed both Donovan and Harald, son of Ivar, then returned to Cashel to prepare himself to meet Molloy, the Owenacht. When he attacked Molloy, he wanted to have all his weapons sharp and his most trusted warriors around him.

Brian's son Murcha met him at the gates of Cashel.

"Is there going to be a big battle and can I take part in it?" the boy asked eagerly. "Look how tall I've grown!"

Brian was surprised to realize Murcha was as long as a spear handle. My son is growing up while I'm kept busy elsewhere, he thought resentfully. He said, "You aren't old enough to take up arms, Murcha."

"But I am—almost," Murcha replied truthfully.

Brian folded his arms and shook his head. He had lost too many people he loved. "You are not going to war yet, and that's final," he told his son.

"But Father . . ."

"Don't argue with me," Brian said, more sharply than he intended.

Murcha turned away as if he had accepted his father's decision, but he had not.

Murcha mac Brian was his father's son. He

longed to be a warrior. From the safety of Cashel he had followed the story of Brian's victories and dreamed of the day when at last he would be allowed to fight with the Dalcassians. He imagined himself riding on a fine horse, as a prince should, following the wind-whipped banner of the three red lions.

When Brian and his warriors left Cashel to seek Molloy of Desmond, Murcha ran beside his father's horse as far as the first crossroads. His dark hair, so like his mother's, was glossy in the sunlight. Brian looked down on it with love. He wanted to tousle that hair, the way Mahon used to tousle his hair. A lump rose in his throat. "Take care of yourself, and your sister and brothers," he told Murcha. Then he kicked his horse and trotted off to battle.

He did not see Murcha falling back and blending in with the other warriors, following him.

The forces of Brian and Molloy met at a place called Bealach Leachta, an ancient battlefield marked by huge stones from a forgotten time. Each side made camp. "This is a good place for the Owenacht to die tomorrow," Brian told his warriors. "It is better than Molloy deserves, for honorable men's bones lie in this soil. Can't you sense them?"

His men shivered in the twilight and looked around them. That night they stayed close to their campfires. But the only spirit that walked the land was that of Brian himself, pacing the borders of the camp and gazing toward the winking red eyes of the Owenacht campfires. "By this time tomorrow," he promised Mahon, "the hand that killed you will be cold."

The battle the next morning was one of the most savage Brian had ever fought. Gael against Gael, the Dalcassians and the Owenachts tried to destroy each other. Each tribe wanted to be supreme in Munster, with its prince at Cashel ruling the rich province. By the end of the day the meadow was littered with bodies. Neither side was willing to surrender.

Among all those furious fighting men, Brian searched in vain for Molloy. The Prince of Desmond was hiding in a hut beyond the edge of the battlefield. When he caught a glimpse of Brian at the start of the battle, his nerve had broken and he had run away.

Brian's son Murcha, who was also trying to hide from his father, had seen Molloy break away from the other warriors and run into the bushes. He did not know it was Molloy, but he followed him. The battle was very loud and very confusing, not quite what he had imagined. Murcha decided it would be easier to fight just one man, at least in his very first combat. If he already had a kill to his credit when Brian found him, perhaps he would be allowed to stay.

Beneath his cloak, Murcha carried a shortsword and had an eager heart.

He followed the other man through a strip of forest, across a stream, and up a slope to a ruined herder's hut. When the man went inside, Murcha crept closer, sword at the ready.

The nearer he got to the hut, the less sure of himself he felt. This was not the glorious battle he had often dreamed. This was two men alone in a wilderness, and the other was a grown man who would surely kill him.

Just as Murcha was beginning to think about turning back, a twig snapped under his foot. The man came out of the hut. "Who's there?" he asked in a loud whisper.

Murcha's mouth was so dry he could not answer. Seeing him, Molloy called, "You there! Lad! Come here to me!"

The Owenacht peered toward Murcha, then suddenly recognized him. This was Brian Boru's son, whom he had seen at Cashel!

A grin split Molloy's face. "You'll be my hostage!" he cried, grabbing Murcha.

Meanwhile, halfway through a long day of battle, someone told Brian his son had been seen, trying to hide among the other warriors. At first Brian did not want to believe it.

"My son had orders to stay at Cashel," he insisted. Even as he said the words, however, he knew how much Murcha was like himself at that age: hungry for adventure and unwilling to follow orders.

Brian was the commander of the Dalcassians and could not be spared to look for Murcha, so he sent others to search and went back to the fighting. It was hard to do. His mind kept skipping away, thinking about Murcha who looked so like his mother.

Beautiful, beloved, dead Mor.

Several times Brian's wandering thoughts almost got him killed. Molloy's men had been ordered to bring down the Prince of Thomond at all costs. As Brian fought with sword and ax he tried not to look at the bodies already lying on the ground, making the grass slippery with blood. He knew one of them might be his oldest son.

Very late in the day, the Dalcassians at last defeated the Owenachts. Molloy's men had not seen their prince since early morning, and without a leader to inspire them they finally surrendered. One by one, they came forward and laid their weapons at Brian's feet. He nodded to each. His shoulders ached and burned from using the sword and the ax, but his heart was more sore still. "Have you seen my son?" he asked again and again.

But no one had.

When Brian's men began recovering bodies from the battlefield, Murcha was not among the dead.

Neither was Molloy, Prince of Desmond.

Although he was bleeding from several wounds, Brian now joined in the search. Darkness was falling when someone saw one figure dragging another out of a strip of woodland. "Look!"

Brian looked. Then weary as he was, he began to run.

When Murcha saw his father coming he dropped the legs of the body he was dragging and stood waiting, trying to look humble and proud at the same time. "I've killed my first man, Father," he said.

Brian wanted to grab his son up in a hug and shout with joy because Murcha was still alive. At the same time, he wanted to take off his belt and beat the boy for frightening him so. Then he looked down at the body of the man Murcha had killed.

It was Molloy of Desmond.

For a few moments, Brian was speechless.

His men quickly gathered around. He knew they would forever judge the quality of his leadership by the way he acted now.

Forcing his voice to be calm and controlled, Brian said, "I congratulate you on your kill. But I must remind you that you disobeyed my orders in coming here. I cannot allow a man who follows my banner to disobey my orders." Brian turned to his old friend Nessa, the slinger. "Take this boy prisoner," he said, "and tie him securely across the back of my horse. We shall take him back to Cashel with us and imprison him there for a seven-night. On bread and water."

Murcha could not believe his ears. He had thought his father would laugh and forgive him, and he would be honored as the hero of the day. After all, he had killed Molloy—though he had not known it was Molloy until he got a good look at the man after striking the fatal blow. A lucky blow, he had to admit to himself.

Now he was being treated like any common warrior who disobeyed orders. As Brian's men took hold of him and began tying his hands and feet he shouted to his father, "I'll never forget this. Nor forgive you!"

"My father's angry because I robbed him of his revenge by killing Molloy myself," Murcha complained to Nessa.

"I wouldn't know about that," Nessa replied. "I just follow orders. There is a lesson for you in that, lad."

Every step the horse took on the journey back to Cashel jolted the breath out of Murcha, who lay tied belly-down across the animal's back. Soon the boy hurt all over. His anger with his father increased until he thought of nothing else. He could barely hear what the warriors nearest him were saying.

"Brian Boru is a hard man but a fair one," they were telling one another. "He did not even give his son special treatment."

"Indeed," one remarked, "and I respect him for that. I would follow him to the gates of hell, myself."

"And I would follow him through them!" boasted another. Everyone laughed—except Murcha.

They returned in triumph to Cashel—except for

Murcha, who was shut away for seven nights and days in a small stone cell with nothing but bread and water to eat and drink.

Now that the Owenacht who had tried to claim the kingship was dead, there was only one man who should follow the slain Mahon as ruler of Munster. Brian's army would accept no one else, and Brian's army was the mightiest in the province.

On the first day of the new moon, Brian Boru was inaugurated King of Munster at Cashel of the Kings. He had spent the night in prayer and fasting under the direction of his brother Marcan. At sunrise he walked through a cheering crowd to the very spot where St. Patrick had once stood.

There the bard of the Dalcassians recited the names of Brian's ancestors to the crowd, to prove he came of a royal line. Then the chief judge of the tribe explained the Brehon law concerning the duties of a king to his land and its people. After the ancient Irish law, the Bishop of Emly blessed Brian in the Christian tradition. The bishop held a gold circlet in one hand and a white rod of authority in the other.

Brian kneeled and laid his sword at the bishop's feet. In return he was given the rod of authority. Then he bowed his head.

The weight of the gold circlet last worn by Mahon settled upon Brian's brow.

Raising his head slowly, Brian stood as tall as he could until he could see beyond the crowd, beyond the wall, to the fertile plains and misty mountains of Munster. All that he saw was beautiful. All that he saw was his to defend and cherish.

Brian closed his eyes, holding the moment.

The spot of earth on which he stood had been sacred for many centuries. Long before Christianity came to Ireland, it had belonged to the old gods of the land. There was power in the earth. Standing there, Brian felt the power rise into him. Suddenly he knew he could do more than be King of Munster. He could do whatever he had the ability to dream.

Brian opened his eyes. He looked again toward the blue mountains and thought of the land that lay beyond them.

Not just Munster.

Ireland.

EIGHT

A Row with Murcha

Murcha was not present when his father was crowned King of Munster. Since being released from his cell he had skulked around the edges of Cashel, avoiding Brian as best he could. He thought he had been very badly treated.

It seemed that all of Munster was singing Brian's praises, but Murcha felt only resentment. He had wanted Brian to praise *him*. Instead, he had been embarrassed in front of the Dalcassians and punished. Not fair, not fair! he kept saying to himself. He spent his time dreaming up schemes for escaping his father's control and becoming his own man.

As soon as Brian was King of Munster, he set about repairing the damage done by recent events. As he told his brother Marcan, "We must put an end to the warring between the tribes. It weakens us. If we had been able to stand together when the first Vikings came to this island, we could have kept them from ever gaining a foothold here.''

The priest wrinkled his forehead. ''If you're thinking of uniting the Irish tribes, Brian, you're dreaming. It's never been done. Every tribe, no matter how small, has its own king and goes its own way.''

The word ''never'' would always be a challenge to Brian Boru. ''If it has never been done,'' he replied, ''then perhaps the time has come to do it.''

He began seeking ways to build new alliances. The slain Prince of Desmond had a son, Cian, who was popular in the south. Unlike his father Molloy, Cian had an open, sunny nature and preferred feasting to plotting. Brian's daughter Sive was too young to marry, but she was not too young to be promised in marriage. She must consent, however, under the old Irish law. So Brian invited Cian to Cashel and encouraged a friendship between the two youngsters.

''If they marry in time, the Dalcassians and the Owenachts will be kin,'' Brian explained patiently to Murcha, who did not like Cian. Murcha had decided he did not like anything Brian did.

Young Cian and Brian Boru got along very well together in fact, and this made Murcha more resentful than ever. He did not understand that Brian was trying very hard to heal the quarrel between the two tribes.

Cian did understand this, and was willing. The promise of being able to marry Sive when she was old enough made him even more willing. "When Sive and I are married the Owenachts and the Dalcassians will be friends instead of enemies," he promised.

Brian grinned and put his arm around the young man. Murcha, watching from a distance, saw this and scowled. "Our father prefers Molloy's son to his own," he complained to his brother Flan.

"He doesn't!"

"You don't understand, Flan," Murcha said. "You're just a little boy." Murcha wanted to make his younger brother feel the jealousy he himself felt.

The new King of Munster worked hard to knit together the tribes of the province, tribes who had never been friends before. He knew how to win on the battlefield. Now he must learn how to win peace for his land. He visited kings who had long been enemies of the Dalcassians and praised their courage, admired their women, their homes and cattle, left gifts in their lodges. From the tributes paid to the King of Munster he set aside funds for rebuilding churches and abbeys that had been destroyed by the Vikings, or damaged by Irish raiders. This won him the support of the clergy.

Brian was successful in winning friends, but he could not win back the love of his son. When he tried to teach Murcha what he himself had learned through experience, he found the boy's mind closed.

"I can't talk to him," Brian complained to Marcan. "Of all my sons, he is the oldest and the one most like me. He is the one I want to have follow me. But he resents everything I do."

"You said it yourself, he is most like you. You would never take orders as a lad, Brian, and neither will your son. You were strong-willed and rebellious and so is he. Give him time and pray over the problem, that is my advice to you."

But the trouble between Brian and Murcha flared into a bitter quarrel when the King of Munster announced he meant to marry again.

"Have you forgotten my mother so soon?" Murcha shouted at Brian in the great hall at Cashel.

"I haven't forgotten Mor at all," Brian replied. How could I, he thought to himself, when I see her in this boy's face?

"Then how can you marry someone else?"

"Listen to me," said Brian, trying to be patient. "I am King of Munster now. It is my duty to make this land prosper. That means I must make it safe from war, because war impoverishes people. So I have chosen Achra of Meath as my wife. Her tribe is connected to the O'Neills, the most powerful tribe in all of Ireland. The High King himself is always chosen from among the O'Neills. Marriage with Achra will give us a small but vital connection to them and allow me to begin extending my influence beyond the borders of Munster."

"You're doing this for the sake of your own ambition!"

"There is nothing wrong with ambition, Murcha, if it isn't selfish. I am ambitious, I admit that, but it's not just for myself. It is also for my people."

"I don't understand you," Murcha said.

"You don't want to understand me. You don't listen to anything I say."

"And why should I?" cried Murcha. "When did you listen to me, or care how I felt?"

"That isn't true," Brian started to say, but Murcha had already turned away.

Over his shoulder the young man shouted back at his father, "I'm leaving Cashel. I'm old enough to look after myself. I don't need anything from you, Brian Boru, and I don't want a new mother!" He stormed out of the hall.

He did not see the pain in his father's eyes.

"Go after him and bring him back," Marcan urged.

"It wouldn't do any good. He would run away again, and resent me all the more." Brian felt as if this latest loss was the worst he had suffered. It hurt so deeply he did not want to talk about it. He clamped his jaw shut and turned his attention to the business of kingship, and the preparations for his marriage to Achra of Meath.

At first Murcha went to the monastic school where he had learned to read and write. The monks made him welcome, but they did not urge him to stay. Brian had recently helped them to build a new chapel and a round tower, and they did not want him to think they were taking Murcha's side. In time the young man drifted on, seeking a place of his own. A place beyond the reach of Brian Boru.

No sooner had Brian wed plump and cheerful Achra, who had gold in her braids and freckles on her nose, than new trouble broke out. Unlike Mor, who was sweet and shy, Achra had a gift for making Brian laugh and he was enjoying a jest of hers in the great hall at Cashel when a messenger came with the news.

In spite of Brian's efforts, not all the tribes of Munster had given him their loyalty. The Deise in the southeast were claiming that the tribute demanded of them was too large. The Danish King of Waterford had learned of this, and with a mixture of threats and promises he set out to make allies of the Deise.

The new alliance between an Irish tribe and a Danish king reached the ears of Donal, the Irish King of Leinster. Leinster and Munster were old enemies. Any weapon that could be used against the strong new King of Munster was welcome news to Donal, who announced he would join with the Deise and the Waterford Danes. Together they would destroy Brian Boru before he gained any more power.

"Who are these Dalcassians, anyway?" Donal demanded to know. "They were an unknown tribe before this Brian Boru. Let them fade back into the mists where they belong!''

Encouraged by such support, the king of the Deise attacked the nearest tribe to his, a tribe loyal to Brian. They sent a cry for help to Cashel. Before the day was over, Brian's army was gathering around the standard of the three red lions.

''Must you go away to battle?'' Achra protested. ''I thought you told me you had made peace in Munster.''

''Peace is never certain when the Danes are stirring up trouble,'' Brian told her. ''Left to themselves, the Deise would not have risen against me. But the Waterford Danes have urged them to it and so I must fight them both. And perhaps Leinster as well,'' he added, with a faraway look in his eyes.

Achra was a wise woman. She studied her new husband, then said, ''I think you want to fight Leinster.''

Brian flashed her a smile. ''Perhaps. To test my strength.''

''But for what reason?''

He did not tell her. Murcha had accused him of ambition. Brian had decided it was wisest to keep his ambitions to himself.

That evening, however, he stood once more on the walls of Cashel and looked out over the land. Over Ireland.

At dawn he led his warriors out to meet the enemy.

Cian of Desmond brought the Owenachts to

fight with Brian. By a series of forced marches, they came up behind the warriors of the Deise, taking them by surprise and winning a major victory. The Deise, together with allies from among the Waterford Danes, and also some of Donal's Leinstermen, fell back to Waterford, seeking protection behind its walls. Brian pursued them and wiped out all pockets of resistance. Then he set off northward to deal personally with the King of Leinster.

Donal was horrified by the size of the army that came marching toward his stronghold at Naas. At first he denied knowing of any plot involving the Deise and the Danes of Waterford. Then Brian led forward the prisoners of war, who included a number of Donal's kinsmen.

With bad grace, Donal was forced to admit, "I sent warriors against you, Dalcassian. I believe you have overstepped yourself and thought it was wise to take a bit out of you."

Brian, who was a head taller than Donal and twenty years younger, smiled. "You are not able to take even a nibble out of me. You are choking on the effort. You wanted to see Leinster superior over Munster, but you shall not see that in my lifetime. And to make certain you remember your error, I shall revive the ancient tribute once claimed against your province by mine for the murder of a southern prince. Each year from now on you are to send to Cashel three hundred horses, three hundred cows, three hundred swords, and three hundred cloaks. You will also acknowledge me as foremost ruler in the south.''

Donal's lips were thin with anger. ''You take a lot on yourself. I suppose you demand marriage with one of my daughters as well? That was part of the ancient tribute, was it not—the King of Munster married a princess of Leinster?''

''I have recently taken a wife,'' Brian replied, ''and so you are excused from that part of the tribute. For now. As long as my woman remains in good health. But you shall deliver the first of it to me at once, as I mean to share it out among my loyal followers.''

Donal was surprised. ''You aren't going to keep it for yourself, then?''

''I am not,'' said Brian Boru.

Donal had no choice but to agree. His stronghold was surrounded by Brian's men, who had arrived before he could summon enough defenders to ward them off. Many of Brian's army rode horses now. The bards claimed the Dalcassian cavalry moved so swiftly the air behind them could not catch up until they halted for the night.

''We shall begin gathering your tribute tomorrow,'' Donal told Brian in a surly tone. ''Enjoy it while you can. Our turn will come.''

Faster than thought, Brian moved. Suddenly the point of a shortsword was pressing into Donal's throat. ''Do not threaten me, Leinster,'' Brian said in a cold and deadly voice. ''Do not ever, ever, threaten me.'

Donal did not say another word until the army of
Munster had disappeared over the horizon. Then he
told his court he had been prevented from speaking
by a sore throat. Most of them seemed to believe
him. He was relieved that the girl called Gormla,
daughter of one of his princely cousins, was not
there, however. She had sharp eyes and would have
seen through the lie, and laughed at him. Gormla
had only contempt for any sort of weakness. But
fortunately she had recently been married to Olaf
Cuaran, the aging Norse King of Dublin.

Donal secretly felt sorry for any man married to
the wild, willful, beautiful Gormla.

NINE

Tribal Warfare

With every season that passed, Brian's goals were expanding. The action of the Waterford Danes in causing a rebellion on the part of the Deise made him more convinced than ever that the power of the foreigners, whether Danish or Norse, must be broken forever in Ireland.

When he was a little boy, Brian had imagined driving all the Vikings into the sea at sword's point. He was older now, and had traveled enough to realize that there were too many Vikings in Ireland to drive all of them into the sea. They must be handled in other ways.

What lessons could be learned from the past? How had great leaders in other lands coped with invasion and settlement by foreigners?

His precious books were always close at hand, and whenever he had the time, Brian studied them. He said to his sons Conor and Flan the words he would have liked to say to Murcha. "Education is priceless. Never stop studying. Books give us access to the finest minds, even those of men long dead."

Brian began sending messengers abroad to buy back the books that had been looted from Ireland's monastic schools and sold to scholars in Europe by Viking traders. Some of the tribute sent by the King of Leinster was used for this purpose.

Some of it was also sent to Murcha, who had at last settled in a small fort of his own a day's ride from Cashel. Murcha did not acknowledge the gift. But he did not send it back, either. Like his father, Murcha was a practical man.

Brian was happy enough with Achra, when he had time to be with her. Achra had very little interest in affairs of kingship. Her world was bound by the child growing inside her and such homely joys as the smell of baking bread and the warmth of a fire. She did not really like Cashel. The cluster of stone buildings jammed together atop the famous rock seemed cold to her, and harsh. The wind was always blowing at Cashel. There were no trees, no flowers. None of the softness of Meath.

She tried to say these things to Brian, but his mind was elsewhere. "I've been studying the annals of the Saxons in England," he told her, "to learn how they made one strong kingdom out of many quarrelsome groups and tribes. Half a century before I was born, a king called Alfred began uniting the tribes of the south under his rule. This pattern has been continued, passed from father to son. The Saxons have created a dynasty bred and trained to rule. Under this dynasty, the Saxons have learned to work together and have made their land prosperous.

"The Danes have begun attacking them, but it seems to me that as long as the Saxons continue to stand together, and have wise warlords to lead them, they can resist.

"I want a similar strength for our land, Achra. I made certain that Murcha received the same education I had, one that would prepare him to rule. Kingship in Ireland has always gone to the strongest, or the one with the most followers, but that isn't good enough. It should follow one dynasty trained for it. One lasting, kingly line. As things are now, the land is divided into many tribal kingdoms and five provinces, and every kingship is fought over again and again. This robs us of our strength and this is what made it easy for the Vikings to overrun us. I want to be certain that such a thing does not happen again. One strong man should rule the entire island, with the support of all its princes."

Brian's eyes flamed with passion. His voice throbbed with strength. Achra clapped her hands and gazed admiringly at her magnificent husband—but she really did not understand him.

Others understood his vision, though. Some were excited by it. Some laughed at it. Some feared it.

In spite of his growing reputation, the princes of the province of Ulster did not yet consider Brian Boru a danger to their own power. For many generations, the high kingship of Ireland—which meant the right to claim tribute from the five provincial kings—had been held in turn by the two senior branches of the O'Neills. The northern O'Neills, whose royal stronghold was at Aileach, did not feel threatened by the rise of some southern warlord from an obscure tribe. Brian had not yet invaded their lands or interfered with their trade.

The southern branch of the O'Neills in Meath were more concerned, however. Munster was too close for comfort, and Brian's marriage to Achra was seen as an attempt to extend his influence.

In the Year of Our Lord 979 the High King, the *Árd Rí* of Ireland, King of the Kings, died. His replacement was chosen from the ranks of the O'Neill princes in Meath.

His name was Malachy the Great.

Malachy had hardly become High King when Olaf Cuaran, the Norse King of Dublin, led an army of plundering Vikings into Meath. Malachy met and defeated them at Tara, which was the ancient ceremonial site of high kingship. Humiliated by this defeat, Olaf Cuaran converted to Christianity, went on an extended pilgrimage to Iona, and died there. He left a young widow, Gormla, the Princess of Leinster.

Following his victory over Olaf Cuaran, Malachy laid siege to Dublin. The Norse trading town was well protected with a stout timber palisade and an army of Viking defenders. But the new High King was eager to make a name for himself. After three days of fierce fighting, he broke down the gates and captured the town.

There he found Donal, King of Leinster. In his bitterness against Brian Boru, Donal had gone to the Norse of Dublin to seek an alliance against Munster. He was the guest of Olaf's son, Sitric Silkbeard, the new King of Dublin.

"I submit to you," Sitric told Malachy, surrendering his sword. "And I promise to pay you a huge tribute in gold and cloth and timber if you allow me to retain the kingship of Dublin."

Malachy agreed. Sitric promptly ordered a feast served in honor of the High King.

One of those attending the feast was Gormla of Leinster, widow of Olaf Cuaran.

Malachy had never seen such a woman. Gormla was as tall as a man, with huge green eyes and hair like flame that fell past her knees. When she met his glance she did not blush and look away. She stared back at him.

"Who is that?" Malachy asked Sitric.

Sitric was called Silkbeard because he was still so young his beard was thin and fine. With boyish pride he told Malachy, "That's my mother. She was a child when she married Olaf Cuaran.''

"She's not a child now,'' Malachy replied, filling his eyes with Gormla.

When he had a chance to speak to her, Malachy was surprised by Gormla's keen interest in politics. She knew a great deal about tribal warfare, and about what was happening in the Irish territories beyond the walls of Dublin.

"The shifts of power are like a chess game, Malachy,'' she said. "I like to play chess myself.''

Turning the full force of her green eyes on the High King, she went on. "Brian Boru of Munster recently humiliated my kinsman, Donal of Leinster. It would make me happy to see the Munster-man paid back in kind. As High King, perhaps you should make some sort of gesture to demonstrate your authority. He is said to be very ambitious and it would not do to have provincial kings think themselves stronger than the High King.''

"I shall do what I can to make the Princess of Leinster happy,'' Malachy replied.

Gormla chuckled.

She thought it a great pity that women could no longer rule their tribes in Ireland. A thousand years earlier, the bards said, Connacht had been controlled by the great Queen Maeve, who started a mighty war.

A war with real men fighting on both sides was much more exciting than chess, Gormla thought. She looked forward to seeing Malachy fight Brian Boru.

At Cashel, Achra had just given birth to a son. He was to be called Teige. Murcha did not attend his half-brother's christening.

While the king's household was celebrating the birth they learned of a shocking deed. Malachy, the new High King, had led an army of warriors from Meath into Thomond and cut down the sacred oak at Magh Adhair. Generations of Dalcassian princes had become kings of the tribe beneath that oak.

Brian was outraged. "What have I done to the High King that gives him cause to insult me and my tribe in this way?"

A new historian had just come to Cashel, a man of the important tribe of Carroll. To this Carroll, Brian said, "Malachy is unfit to be High King. He acts unjustly, attacking without cause. Even worse, he has profaned a site sacred to our tribe."

Carroll was a round-faced man with the piercing blue eyes common to his branch of the tribe in Kerry. It would be his business to observe Brian's deeds and write them down for future generations, so he was interested in the twists and turns of Brian's mind. "Will you seek revenge?" he asked.

"I don't believe in revenge," Brian replied. "It is not Christian."

Then he winked. And Carroll was not sure just what Brian Boru believed.

First Brian sent his boats up and down the Shannon, packed with armed warriors. The Irish were accustomed to seeing Vikings on the river, but not men of their own race. The lesson was not lost on them. Brian was asserting his power. The leaders of tribes from both banks of the Shannon hurried to send tributes to Brian and dispatched warriors to join his army.

When he had enough men, Brian marched into Meath and laid waste to a large area. His banner with its crimson lions was planted defiantly deep in Malachy's home territory.

In his stronghold at the Fort of the Swords, Malachy was taken aback. He had not expected such a bold response. The High King had only meant to make a gesture, not an enemy. But he was in no position to reply in kind, for he had a new war on his hands. Young Sitric Silkbeard had joined forces with the King of Leinster and the two were attacking Meath on the east.

When Malachy destroyed the Dalcassians' sacred tree at Magh Adhair, he had pleased Gormla, but he had not impressed Donal of Leinster. To him, the gesture seemed an empty threat. The King of Leinster was convinced that the Vikings were the greatest power in Ireland, and that his prosperity depended on alliance with them.

Malachy marched into Leinster to meet Donal and Sitric. A savage battle took place. At last Malachy won, but he did not follow up his victory by destroying Sitric. The young man was allowed, for the sake of his mother Gormla, to return safely to Dublin. There he waited, bitter and brooding, for a better opportunity.

Within a short time Donal of Leinster was slain

in a petty dispute with another Irish tribe.

The next important King of Leinster was to be Maelmora, a brother to the princess Gormla.

Gormla persuaded Malachy to support her brother's bid for the provincial kingship. For a while, Gormla could persuade Malachy to do almost anything. She had arranged to be present at almost every feast and fair the High King attended, and soon he was thinking about her all the time. He told his followers, "If I marry Olaf Cuaran's widow, I will gain two alliances—one with Sitric Silkbeard and the Norsemen of Dublin, and one with the kingly line of Leinster."

So Malachy asked Gormla to marry him, and to no one's surprise she accepted. She was bored with being a widow. Being the wife of a king, particularly the High King, should be much more exciting.

But Malachy was not a good judge of character. In spite of his mother's marriage, Sitric had no desire to make peace with Malachy again. He resented being defeated by Malachy. Besides, there was still plunder to be taken in Meath.

As for Maelmora of Leinster, his only interest was in promoting his own career. He would give his loyalty wherever he thought it would do him the most good.

Meanwhile, Malachy kept hearing more and more about the increasing strength of Brian Boru. Bards visiting the Fort of the Swords sang songs praising the Lion of Thomond. Sometimes they even played airs on the harp that, they said, had been composed by Brian.

Gormla looked at her second husband through narrowed eyes. "Can you compose music for the harp?" she wanted to know.

"Of course not. I'm a warrior, a king."

"So is Brian Boru," Gormla commented. She closed her eyes and listened with increasing interest to the harp music. The King of Munster must be an interesting man, she began thinking. It had not taken her long to grow bored with Malachy.

Gormla told her husband, "I hear that Brian Boru is building a new stronghold for himself at a place called Kincora, the head of the Weir, near where he was born. It is said to be a fortress that will put your fort to shame."

Malachy snorted. "A palace in a wilderness. Ruled over by an upstart savage."

"Savages do not read and write Latin and Greek," Gormla pointed out. "They say this Brian Boru does both. And excels at chess," she added dreamily.

Malachy lost his temper. "Enough! I do not want to hear the Dalcassian's name spoken in my house again!"

But Gormla was not good at taking orders. She avidly collected every scrap of information about the activities of the King of Munster.

She learned that Brian was not a king who lingered comfortably in his hall, feasting and drinking, as Malachy liked best to do. Brian went out among his people, listened to their complaints, tried to solve their problems. Kings were usually jealous of their position. But Brian Boru would sit cross-legged on the dirt floor of the meanest hut to discuss a barren ewe with a herder, or an outbreak of disease among her children with the herder's wife.

He would then send a new ewe from his own flock, and his own physician to heal the children.

Brian Boru was uniting his people through their admiration rather than their fear.

Malachy did not inspire such devotion, Gormla observed. He was a fine warrior, but compared to the King of Munster he seemed a very ordinary man.

Brian's wife Achra bore him two sons, then died in childbirth as a daughter was born. When she learned of this, Gormla remarked to one of her attendants, "Brian Boru will be High King one day. He will need another wife then, to give him the benefit of her advice and comfort and to share in his glory. I would make a good wife for him, would I not?"

The attendant was shocked. "You're already married!"

"And Malachy is the High King. For now. But things change. Under the old Brehon law, for example, a husband or wife can be set aside."

"The Church does not believe in divorce," her attendant pointed out.

"Perhaps not, but the priests overlook many of

the things kingly families do. The Church depends on the kings for support and protection.''

The attendant said, ''No woman would divorce a High King!''

''Perhaps not. But the High King might divorce a woman who no longer pleased him,'' Gormla replied, smiling a secret smile.

Before she could develop her plans, however, Brian married again.

Aside from Murcha, no one was surprised when he took a daughter of King Conor of Connacht as his third wife. Munster and Connacht had fought many battles, but now Connacht would be bound to Brian through ties of marriage.

Brian did not take his new wife, Ducholi, to live at Cashel. Instead they made their home at Kincora, on the west bank of the Shannon, in the heart of Thomond. Brian had fortified Beal Boru to serve as its northern rampart, built additional walls extending southward for two miles, and erected a magnificent new hall on the high ground. From this vantage point he could view with satisfaction the fleet of three hundred boats he had assembled on the Shannon.

Once Kincora was completed, Brian visited the Rock of Cashel only for ceremonial occasions. Afterward he hurried eagerly back to his home on the Shannon, beneath the watchful eye of Aval on her gray crag.

Ducholi was a slender, graceful woman, with a taste for luxury. She had not been long at Kincora before she began using part of the tribute sent to the King of Munster to add the gleam of gold to her new home. She ordered fine cups and bowls made by the craftsmen of Thomond, and no gown that she wore was worth less than six cows.

Brian was quietly pleased by the changes Ducholi made, turning a fortress into a palace. He told his personal bard, Mac Liag, "I wish my mother had lived to see this place. She had a hard life and died a hard death."

Brian kept his voice steady as he spoke, but Mac Liag had a keen ear. He heard the grief buried in the words.

"After my mother's death," Brian went on, "I promised myself I would do what I could to see that such things did not happen again."

Mac Liag said, "You have succeeded. No Viking would dare attack any part of the Shannon now."

Brian sighed. "That isn't enough."

Mac Liag had a home by the shores of Lough Derg, just north of Beal Boru. Daily he walked to Brian's hall to share the king's cup, his joys and his sorrows. The two men became the best of friends. Brian did not want to talk about war and warfare all the time, and Mac Liag was an educated man who could discuss many subjects with him. Sometimes the two sat deep in conversation in the hall until dawn.

Brian confided to Mac Liag, "The defeat that hurts me most is the loss of my son Murcha."

"You've healed so many other quarrels. Can't you heal this one?"

"I've tried," Brian said. "And to Murcha's credit, he behaves toward me as a loyal prince to his king. But he allows nothing personal between us. When we meet, he treats me as a stranger."

"Why?"

The fire was burning low in the huge stone firepit in the center of the hall. Brian's hounds dozed beside the hearth, twitching in their sleep. His servants lay under tables or in corners, sleeping as soundly as the dogs. Only Brian and Mac Liag were still awake.

Brian rubbed the bridge of his nose with weary fingers. "I don't know why, Mac Liag. Perhaps there's always trouble between fathers and sons. I know Murcha resents my marriages since his mother died. He refuses to understand the reason for them. He refuses to accept my idea of kingship, though I have tried and tried to teach him."

Mac Liag leaned back on his bench, resting his spine against the stout wooden pillar that helped support the roof. Lacing his fingers across his belly, the bard told Brian, "Time is passing, and we're all getting older. Even Murcha. He also has a wife now, and a child on the way, we hear. So perhaps he would be more willing to listen to you if the two of you would talk together again."

"We won't. He avoids me. And I'm not about to plead, not to my son or any man!"

Mac Liag said nothing more about Murcha, but stared at the fire, thinking.

The next morning he sought out Carroll the historian, whom he found in Brian's huge new wine cellar, across the river from Kincora. The cellar was necessary to store the immense tribute of wine Brian was demanding from the Danes of Limerick, in return for letting them rebuild their town.

Winter had clamped its cold grip on Thomond. The reed-fringed hem of Lough Derg was spangled in ice. Daily, hunters left Kincora and the surrounding area, where Brian had almost three thousand warriors encamped at all times, to seek game for the approaching Christmas feasting.

Brian's wife, Ducholi, was spending much time in the kitchens of Kincora, supervising preparations. Women worked red-faced, loading and unloading the round clay ovens. Men worked red to the elbow, cutting up beef and venison. Servants ran back and forth endlessly from kitchen to hall. Built to the king's own clever design, the kitchens were connected to the feasting hall by two separate passages, so servants could carry food in or empty dishes away without running into one another.

Children were collecting nuts, young girls were hanging swags of evergreen boughs, musicians were tuning harps and burnishing trumpets. In the still of the night they played instruments called musical branches, whose tiny silver bells filled the hall with a sound like icicles breaking.

Everyone was in a fever, preparing for Christmas.

Carroll the historian was busily writing down, on a wax tablet, the measurements of Brian's new wine cellar, and dreaming of the wine he would drink during the festive season. He did not notice Mac Liag approach until the bard said, "You know Murcha, don't you?"

Startled, Carroll dropped his wax tablet. Mac Liag waited while he picked it up.

"I do know the Prince Murcha, slightly," Carroll said.

"Do you think he regrets the break with his father?"

"I'm sure he does," the historian said. "Murcha is a good man at heart, and he loves his father. He just won't admit it. It must be very difficult, having Brian Boru for a father. He is a hero to so many, and Murcha has never been comfortable standing in his shadow."

"Brian misses his son, Carroll. But he won't make the first move. He has settled so many disputes for others—do you think you and I might try to help with this one?"

The historian looked doubtful. "I suppose we could try," he said at last.

Together, they went to Murcha's fort, to issue an invitation in both their names. "As senior prince of the senior line of the Dalcassians, you should be at the king's table for the Christmas feast," Carroll urged.

Murcha started to refuse, but his wife said suddenly, in a wistful voice, "Christmas at Kincora! Wouldn't that be splendid? Ah, my husband—what I would give to see it."

"It will be splendid," Mac Liag quickly echoed. Murcha shot him a warning look that he ignored. "A thousand beeswax candles will burn brighter than the sun. There will be more fat meat than any man can lift on his knife. The abbot Marcan will be coming from the new abbey that Brian built for him, and would surely bless the child in your womb."

The young woman turned to her husband with such a pleading look Murcha could not refuse. Over her head, he glared at his visitors. "You are as full of schemes as my father," he said.

Then he smiled a rueful smile. "Get your cloak from its peg, wife. It appears we are going to spend Christmas at Kincora."

TEN

Christmas at Kincora

As Mac Liag had promised, Christmas at Kincora in the Year of Our Lord 994 was indeed a splendid occasion. Ducholi was a daughter of the King of Connacht. She knew that a king must display his wealth to impress his people with his ability to take care of them.

"The bards praise a king's hospitality first among his qualities," Ducholi kept reminding the servants. "My husband's victories in battle mean that many new tribes now send him tribute. He likes to claim that every back in Munster now wears a new cloak. I should like to be able to claim that, at this feast, we stretched every belly to bursting!"

The servants did their best.

Brian's cooks prepared a new dish in honor of their king. This Dalcassian stew simmered in huge iron cauldrons until its fragrance made everyone's mouth water. It contained many of the foods available to noble households in Ireland at that time. Mutton, duck, bacon, venison, sausage, barley, wild onions, and root vegetables were cooked together, then flavored with dried herbs, imported cinnamon, and the dregs of red wine. The Dalcassian recipe would be served for many years after in Thomond, with shellfish and cresses added during the summer, and those who tasted it remembered the name of Brian Boru.

Years later, Prince Cahal of Delvin Mor told his many grandchildren, "I was there at Kincora, when we drank from silver cups."

"Tell us!" the children would demand. They never tired of hearing the tale.

Cahal's eyes would grow misty with remembering. "The great feasting hall at Kincora was built of timber, with a roof as high as the treetops. Brian Boru sat on a raised platform facing the main doorway, with his nobles around him according to their rank. Those of us who could command more than a hundred men in time of battle sat closest to the king. Farthest away were cattle lords who only held land to the value of fourteen cumals, which means fourteen servant women. Such men sat in the shadows and the drafts but they ate as much as the rest of us. And drank more," Cahal would add with a laugh.

"And what did the great king look like?" the children wanted to know.

"Ah, Brian was in his prime in those days! There were the first streaks of silver in his coppery hair, but he had the eyes of a boy. Not a boy . . . an eagle! He was a head taller than the tallest of us, and no man in Munster could match him with sword or ax. His voice was deep and seldom used, for he listened much more than he talked. I used to watch him across the feasting table and wonder how many thoughts were flashing through his mind at the one time."

"Were you his special friend?"

Cahal smiled. "Every man thought he was Brian Boru's special friend. He had that gift. He never betrayed a friendship, or gave any man cause to regret trusting him. Though we came from many tribes, somehow Brian Boru made us all Dalcassians.

"Another of his gifts was his memory. He knew the Book of Rights, the ancient laws of Ireland, as well as any man living. He could recite the poems containing the law and he knew how to interpret them," Cahal added, recalling the many times Brian had interpreted the law to suit his own purpose.

That Christmas at Kincora, Brian had been thankful to see Murcha enter the main gateway with his other guests. He wanted to run up to him and make him welcome, but he held himself back. What if Murcha turned away from his father?

So Brian just smiled and nodded at his oldest son as he did at everyone. But he ordered his steward to give Murcha the seat at his right hand during the feast.

To Brian's relief, Murcha accepted it.

Both men were wary, careful with each other. They spoke of little things that did not matter. Perhaps it will be all right, Brian thought to himself. Murcha has come to me of his own free will. Perhaps he is ready to listen and learn.

After the feast, the musicians played music at the king's request, while Brian's shaggy hounds roamed through the feasting hall, nosing among the rushes on the floor for scraps and bones. Then Brian raised his hand to order silence. It was time to address his followers.

"I am troubled by the actions of the High King Malachy," he said. "A High King should be the man who is best equipped for the office, a man who desires to improve the lot of his people. The great King Charlemagne of France, whose life I have studied, was such a man.

"Malachy is not such a man. He is content to enjoy the privileges of his rank and demand submission and tributes. But there is more to kingship than taking tributes.

"I know more of the law than Malachy does. There is nothing in the law that gives the O'Neill tribe a claim on the high kingship forever. They took it through force of arms, and they can lose it the same way." Brian cast a meaningful look around the room, then met and held the eyes of his oldest son.

Murcha slouched low on his bench. Out of the side of his mouth he said to the man sitting on his right, "My father is lecturing me again."

That man was Cahal of Delvin Mor, who replied, "You would be wise to listen to him. He is trying to prepare you for kingship."

"He wants to be more than King of Munster," said Murcha. "Listen to him. He plans to be High King."

"And why not?" asked Cahal.

Why not indeed? thought Murcha for the first time, looking at his father with new eyes. Perhaps Brian Boru should become High King. But if he does—what about his son? Will I still, and always, stand in his shadow?

Murcha remained at Kincora for the twelve nights of celebration, and went home full of thoughts. As Mac Liag had told Brian, Murcha was growing older and wiser. He would always have a quick temper, however.

People far beyond Thomond were beginning to ask, "Why shouldn't Brian Boru be High King? He does more for his followers than Malachy does for his."

Brian was making it obvious that he would not submit to the authority of a High King he did not respect. Munster and Meath clashed again and again in small battles. But Brian was unwilling to declare a total war. He did not want his rivalry with

Malachy to ravage the very land he hoped to win. Nor did he want great numbers of his followers killed. He was concerned for the lives of his people, and they knew it.

Even Murcha had to admit to himself that Brian was a superb king.

Malachy was being forced to admit it as well. He forbade his bards to sing of Brian, yet the name was on everyone's lips.

Gormla said it once too often. Malachy turned on her in a fury in their chamber at the Fort of the Swords.

"I'm tired of hearing that name! Mention Brian Boru once more, wife, and sleep beneath another roof!"

Gormla gave her husband a scornful look. Malachy, who was several years younger than Brian, was as bald as if he had a monk's tonsure. His belt was straining against a growing belly. He was not a man to stir the imagination.

Gormla was tired of him.

"Boru, Boru, Boru!" she chanted.

A messenger arrived at the gates of Dublin and asked to be taken to King Sitric. He found Sitric in the street of the leatherworkers, ordering new boots for himself.

The messenger told him, "Your mother, the Princess Gormla, wishes you to know that the High King has set her aside. She is no longer his wife."

Sitric raised his sandy-colored eyebrows. He was very fair, like his Norse father. The Irish called the Norse "white foreigners" and the darker Danes "black foreigners."

"What?" asked Sitric, not certain he had heard right. "Are you trying to tell me the High King has divorced my mother?"

"Under the Brehon law, he has. She wants you to take her in and give her a home."

Sitric forgot about boots. He was young but not stupid. He knew Gormla, in spite of her beauty, was a troublemaker. She had always been a troublemaker. Gormla could not pass a pot without stirring it up.

"I'm not certain Dublin is the best place for my mother at present," Sitric said to the messenger. "She might be better advised to take shelter with her brother Maelmora, the King of Leinster. After all, she persuaded Malachy to support him for the kingship. Maelmora owes her a favor."

The messenger was surprised. One did not expect a son to refuse a home to his own mother. But he carried Sitric's words back to the Fort of the Swords, where Gormla was now living in a small lodge apart from the main buildings. When she heard what Sitric had said, her howls of anger echoed through the fort.

Malachy was away at the time, putting down a revolt by one of the tribal kings. Though Gormla had secretly wanted to be free of him, she publicly pretended to be very angry about the divorce. It was an insult, she told everyone who would listen.

She had looked forward to complaining bitterly to her son, Sitric.

Maelmora, her brother, was a different matter. She knew him of old; he had no patience with her and would not be willing to give ear to her moans. They did not get along.

But Sitric sent word to Maelmora that he must, indeed, offer Gormla a home. "Do this and you shall have an alliance with me and the Norsemen of Dublin," Sitric promised.

Maelmora was new to the kingship of Leinster and eager for powerful alliances, and so he agreed. He sent an escort of warriors to bring his sister home.

"We shall only keep her here until we find a new husband for her," Maelmora promised his wife.

"See that you do," said the wife, pursing her lips. She did not get along with Gormla either.

In the winter of 998, smoke hung without moving in the cold air and snagged like wool in the leafless branches of the trees. Then a cold rain set in, lasting for weeks.

Brian paced the halls of Kincora, thinking. Winter was the time for thinking. The land demanded a rest, and made it all but impossible for men to wage war because of mud and sleet and ice. In winter a warrior stayed home by his fire, repairing his weapons and renewing his courage.

As King of Munster, Brian formally summoned Murcha. In the great hall of Kincora he said to his oldest son, "You are a prince of the Dalcassians with more than a hundred warriors sworn to you. I ask you to bring them to me in the springtime."

"You're going to war then?"

"I am."

"Are you going to try to kill the High King?"

"I am not. I would not have the bards remember me as one who did harm to a High King."

"Then who is to receive our spear throws and sword thrusts?" Murcha wanted to know. "Whose blood will we feed to the ravens?"

Brian did not answer at once. Instead, he signaled to a servant to poke up the fire in the central firepit. A bitter wind was howling beyond the walls.

Gazing into the leaping flames, Brian said at last, "When I was your age, Murcha, I thought all our problems would be solved if we drove the foreigners into the sea. I was young and things seemed simple. I have lived long and observed much, and now I know better.

"Many of our problems come from ourselves, not from the foreigners. Besides, there are too many Norse and Danes here now to drive them all out, and they have been here for too long. For generations. They have married Irish women and they have children who were born here and know no other home. I would not drive any child from its home, Murcha. Not ever.

"Some of the Vikings have even become Christians. They are part of the pattern of this island now. Look at the carving on that leather belt you wear. Those are Viking figures mixed with the Irish knotwork. And tonight in the feasting hall we shall fill our cups with Danish beer.

"Look hard at the servants who bring it, for some of them contain Viking blood. Yet I trust them with the treasures of Kincora."

A muscle knotted in Brian's jaw. The next words were hard for him to say aloud, but he must say them and Murcha must listen and understand.

"We cannot drive the foreigners out, my son. They are here to stay, part of us and part of this land. They must be won to our side as I won the tribes of Munster. They must realize that they are now Irish, too, and learn to love this land as we love her. We must forge one huge tribe out of all these parts, and teach that tribe not to savage itself."

Murcha was staring at his father. "You are mad."

Ignoring him, Brian said, "We cannot win a man like Sitric Silkbeard, however. He is hard and cruel, a Viking to his soul, and the worst sort of Viking. He wants only to seize and smash. And he has an ally of the same nature now, Maelmora of Leinster. They have begun plundering the tribes along the coast and dividing the spoils."

At last Murcha thought he saw where all this was leading. "You're going to war against Sitric and Maelmora!"

"I am. But not alone. I want to put together an

army large enough to discourage such partnerships of greed now and in the future. And for that I need a new ally.

"Murcha," said Brian, "I want you to go with me to meet the High King, and ask him to join forces with the army of Munster to fight Sitric and Maelmora."

Murcha fumbled for a bench and sat down. Hard. "But I thought Malachy was your enemy!"

"He isn't my enemy, Murcha. He is my rival. Don't be too quick to call anyone an enemy, particularly if he is born in the same land as yourself. There are few enough of us as it is. We cannot afford to be enemies; is that not what I was just saying?

"The High King and I would be better served by standing together at this time, and I want you with me when I go to convince him. It will be a valuable lesson for you."

Still sitting on his bench, Murcha twisted his neck to look up, up, up at Brian, towering above him. "I cannot believe you want me on such a mission, Father. Nothing I've ever done has been good enough for you. What if I should say or do the wrong thing this time?"

"Then we shall both learn a lesson," said Brian Boru.

ELEVEN

Allies

When spring came, Malachy was reported to be somewhere north of Clonmacnois, collecting tributes. Brian and Murcha, with an army of Munstermen, set out to find him. As they rode side by side, Murcha kept glancing at Brian out of the corner of his eye. How could anyone live up to such a father?

Brian sat tall and easy on his horse. The animal was a spirited bay stallion with prancing gaits and a tossing head, but Brian handled him with no difficulty. In the Irish fashion he used a single rein attached to a leather headcollar, and carried a horsegoad in one hand to urge his mount forward.

Brian, Murcha observed, rode as if he had been born on a horse. His own horse gave a sudden start, nearly throwing him to the ground. Brian looked over and grinned.

He is laughing at me, Murcha thought bitterly. He never did think I could ride, though he taught me.

They rode on in silence.

Malachy was astonished to learn that an army was approaching from the south. No scouts had warned him of Brian's advance until the Munstermen were almost upon him. This could only mean that Brian Boru had somehow brought many warriors a long distance without being betrayed by the tribes whose land they crossed.

The High King did not like to think that another king commanded such loyalty.

Hastily gathering his own warriors, Malachy marched to intercept Brian on the shores of Lough Ree.

To Malachy's surprise, the King of Munster arrived under a flag of truce. A messenger sent from Brian to the High King's tent announced, "Brian Boru requests hospitality from Malachy."

Such a request must be honored, always. Besides, Malachy was eager to meet Brian face to face. He wanted to see if the fabled Lion of Thomond lived up to his legend.

When Brian arrived at his tent Malachy realized the legends were true. The Dalcassian was a giant. The very way he carried himself marked him as a king, and the scars on his face and arms marked him as a warrior.

In spite of himself, Malachy was impressed. He ordered his servants to bring warm water, according to custom, so his guest could bathe his face and feet. Then he showed Brian to a stool inside his leather tent.

Malachy began by asking, "Why have you come here?" He was very suspicious.

Brian smiled as if they were old friends. "To offer you an opportunity, of course."

"What?"

"The army of Munster plans to challenge the alliance between Dublin and Leinster. It is a threat to our own tribes in the east. I have come to invite you to join with us and share in the spoils."

Malachy was too startled to answer at once.

Fighting the Danes in the hills of Clare, Brian had long ago learned the value of surprise. While the High King was trying to collect his thoughts, Brian went on, "Of course if you and your warriors don't want to join us, we shall fight on our own. We have more than enough men to win a victory without you." He stood up as if he were going to leave.

Forcing himself to think fast, Malachy realized this must mean that Brian had a huge army indeed. Larger than he had ever realized. An army large enough to challenge the High King himself, perhaps. An army large enough to claim the high kingship and all the tributes that involved.

Yet instead Brian was offering Malachy this one chance to be his ally.

Without thinking any further, Malachy said hastily, "Of course we shall stand with you! I have been planning to do the same thing myself. Sit down again and take wine with me, and let's discuss combining our forces."

While the two kings were inside the tent, a company of Brian's Munstermen waited outside. Malachy's Meathmen eyed them curiously. One, they noted, a tall, dark-haired man, was dressed as a prince and wore a gold torc around his neck.

Murcha had placed himself nearest the opening of the tent, so he would be the first to see his father's face when Brian came out.

Brian caught his son's eye and gave a wink, so quick no one else noticed it.

As they returned to the army of Munster, Murcha asked his father, "Do we have enough men to defeat Leinster and Dublin?"

"We do now," said Brian Boru.

Murcha never knew how to feel about his father. Sometimes he hated him. Sometimes he loved him.

In this moment of success, Brian Boru looked almost like a boy again, with sparkling eyes and a smile splitting his red-gold beard.

Malachy had been rushed into making a promise without time for thought, which was just what Brian had intended. Only afterward did the High King realize that the King of Munster meant to give the orders to their combined armies himself. Worse still, Malachy discovered that both sets of warriors were willing to follow him without question. They considered it an honor to follow the standard of the Lion of Thomond.

Brian had stolen the High King's authority through the force of his personality and his fame.

In the Year of Our Lord 999, Sitric and Maelmora were openly plundering the lands west of Dublin. Brian marched his army out of Munster to challenge them, as if he meant to lay siege to Dublin. Malachy brought his own army out of Meath and the two joined forces in the hills beyond the Viking town.

When the High King arrived he learned that Brian had never intended to lay siege to Dublin. Instead, he planned to lure the enemy into a clever trap at a place called Glenn Mauma, where the shape of the land gave his army an advantage. The site was easy to defend, a valley rising at one end toward the slopes of Saggart.

Unknowingly, Sitric and Maelmora led their army into this trap. A savage battle followed. By the end of the bloodstained day, more than four thousand of the Dubliners and their Leinster allies lay dead.

Fleeing for his life, Maelmora hid himself in the branches of a yew tree. There he was found at the sunset hour by some of Murcha's men. Brian's son personally dragged the King of Leinster out of the tree, with grim satisfaction.

Murcha took Maelmora to the command tent. "I bring you this one alive, Father," he said. "I haven't killed him as I did Molloy of Desmond. He is yours to kill."

Brian looked at the King of Leinster. Maelmora was a wiry, agile man, with eyes like two chips of flint. He spat at Brian in defiance, but Brian could smell the fear on him.

Together with Malachy, the leaders of the winning side were crowding around the command tent. Everyone wanted to see Maelmora pay the price. Sitric had successfully escaped to Dublin, so the King of Leinster must bear the full weight of punishment.

Slowly, Brian sheathed his sword. "I'm not going to kill Maelmora," he announced. "He is a prince of the Gael. He is one of us."

A gasp of shock rippled through the crowd. Malachy's face turned red. "You're making a terrible mistake! Why else did we fight? Had you met this man on the field of battle you would have struck him down. I myself saw you kill at least a dozen in single combat."

"I did," Brian agreed gravely. "But now the fighting is over. So let us be done with it."

The day had been long and the fighting had been fierce. Brian had himself killed more than any other warrior at Glenn Mauma. His shoulders ached from swinging the ax. Hot pains shot up his wrists from using his huge two-handed sword, larger and heavier than any other man could manage.

Looking at Maelmora, Brian thought to himself:

All that butchery has led to this. One frightened man shivering with fear in the twilight, while other men watch with blood-lust in their eyes.

"I give you your life," he said to Maelmora, who was at first too dazed to understand.

"You fool!" Murcha burst out. "Do you think Maelmora will thank you for sparing him? He will have nothing but contempt for you, and kill you when he gets a chance!"

Malachy agreed. "I was married to Maelmora's sister. I know from experience, they are cubs from a savage litter. Kill this man while you can, Brian, or you must forever guard your back against him. You can't trust a Leinsterman."

"We have to trust," Brian said simply. "And it might as well begin here. Don't mistake compassion for weakness, however. A truly strong man doesn't kill an opponent when he has him helpless."

"This isn't your decision to make!" Malachy cried. "I am the High King, remember!"

Brian held out his sword to Malachy. "Then kill him yourself. Kill him here and now, in front of all these men, while he kneels on the ground in terror, beaten and helpless. Show us how strong you are, Malachy. Show these men that no mercy can be expected from you as High King."

Malachy was a strong man, but he did not dare try to use Brian's huge sword. He stood, uncertain what to do, while Brian turned on his heel and went into the command tent.

Malachy looked at Murcha. "How can I argue with him?"

"I've tried all my life to argue with him," Murcha replied. "And never won."

"But I am High King!" Malachy protested again.

The other men merely looked at him. The real power had gone with Brian Boru into the tent, and they knew it.

Crouching on the earth, Maelmora knew it, too.

Sitric stayed in Dublin only long enough to collect his valuables. Rightly guessing that Malachy and Brian would now loot and burn the town, he fled northward seeking safety.

The thousands of warriors who had followed Brian and Malachy expected the reward of plunder for their efforts, and they were not disappointed. The loot Brian had once found in Limerick did not compare with the treasure stored in Dublin. The Vikings had a vast trade network; not all of the wealth in Sitric's storehouses had been stolen from the Irish.

Malachy claimed, "I am High King, so my men should have the larger portion."

"Your men fought no harder than mine," Brian reminded him.

Malachy decided the time had come to assert himself.

"I claim my share, and also the tribute you owe me as King of Munster. A large portion of your spoils must go to your High King."

In his deep, slow voice, Brian said, "I don't consider you my High King, Malachy. You are not superior to me. And you have done no more than any of my men who fought and risked their lives. I shall not give the plunder they earned to you."

"You must!" cried Malachy. "If you refuse, I shall attack you with the armies of Ulster and Leinster and Connacht and . . ."

Brian smiled. "The princes of northern Ulster would not come this far unless there was something in it for them. Will you give them your plunder? And you know the Leinstermen would not stand with you, not after this. As for Connacht, I am married to the king's daughter; he would not send you warriors to use against me. You cannot threaten me, Malachy. I am stronger than you."

How did this happen? Malachy was asking himself. He had a dreadful idea. "Do you desire to be High King yourself, Brian Boru? Is that what this is really about? Do you mean to try to seize Tara?"

Brian opened his eyes very wide, as if such a thought had never been in his head. "Why would I seize Tara? I have the kingly seat at Cashel and my own fine home at Kincora. I shall be going there tomorrow. I am tired of war. I want to see my family, and fish at the weir, and take my hounds hunting."

And so he did.

TWELVE

Gormla

As part of his share of the plunder of Dublin, Brian took Viking weapons and armor home to his sons and gold jewelry home to his daughters. He offered Murcha the pick of the loot, but his oldest son was angry again and the gesture did not win him over.

"You should have killed Maelmora," he said bitterly.

"Perhaps. But that was for me to decide, not you. And you should not have called me a fool in front of others, Murcha," Brian replied. He was tired of holding his temper with his son.

"I think you are a fool if you believe you can let that man live and not expect him to put a knife in your back someday."

"Listen to me, Murcha." Brian resolved to try one more time. "Leinster and Munster have been enemies for as long as the bards can remember. I want to end the battles between our two provinces if I can."

"Why?"

"Because I don't like to see Irish men killing Irish men."

"But they always have done, Father."

"That is not a good enough reason!"

Brian despaired of making Murcha understand. No one could see the vision he saw, of a land where men worked together instead of tearing each other apart. It could be done, he knew. Other lands had ended their tribal warfare and become stronger as a result. Once even Rome had been only a savage collection of quarrelsome tribes. Under strong leadership, however, Rome had become an empire.

An empire.

Sometimes Brian climbed alone to the windy heights of the gray crag, and whispered the word to Aval.

Empire.

When Brian left Dublin, Malachy also went home, back to Meath. He gave a great feast and invited all his tribal kings to help him celebrate the victory. While they still sat at the feasting board, word came that Brian had sent messengers to Sitric Silkbeard. Sitric was hiding in Ulster, but somehow Brian had learned where he was. He had demanded that Sitric give to him the formal surrender of Dublin.

"I should have been the one to make that demand!" cried the High King. But the truth is, he had not thought of it.

His alarm increased when he learned that Sitric had returned to Dublin. Brian allowed him to do so on condition that Sitric accept the King of Munster as overlord of the town.

Sitric was no fool. Dublin was the hub of a large and profitable trade network he did not want to lose. He saw that if he meant to regain his position there, he must make peace with the King of Munster. In the complicated tangle of Irish kings and princes, Brian Boru was the strongest.

Sitric did not return alone to Dublin. He had his trusted Viking bodyguards with him, and he was met outside the gates by his mother, Gormla.

"My brother Maelmora is like a beaten hound," Gormla told Sitric. "He slouches around his stronghold snarling, and whining about Brian Boru. I cannot stand him any longer. You must take me in."

Sitric gave his mother a long, thoughtful look. She was still beautiful. The years seemed to have little power over her. Her face was strong and proud, and time had not tarnished the glory of her red hair.

She might be useful, Sitric thought.

Aloud he said, "Of course you are welcome,

Mother. Come with me and make Dublin your home."

Gormla hesitated. "Is this the same son who insisted I live with Maelmora after that wretched Malachy set me aside?"

"I never insisted, Mother. I only suggested. You always said I was a coarse Viking like my father, so I thought you would be more comfortable in your brother's Gaelic household."

"Your father was never so careful of my feelings," said Gormla. "Olaf Cuaran treated me like one of his servants. He was always accusing me of plotting against him, as I recall."

"And were you?"

"Of course not!" Gormla said. But there was a twinkle in her eye. "Ah, perhaps I was. Just a little. But we women are such weak, helpless creatures, we have to better our positions in any way we can."

Sitric snorted. "I know you, Mother. No less weak and helpless creature ever walked the earth. I suspect you caused as much trouble to the High King as you did to my father, and Malachy had to divorce you to save himself from your scheming."

Gormla shrugged. "I wanted him to give me my freedom, if truth be told. I was tired of him. There are better fish in the lake than Malachy."

"Have you someone in mind?"

Gormla smiled and lowered her eyelids, so he could not read her eyes. "Perhaps I have, Sitric. Perhaps I have. I've been thinking . . ."

"I suspect you and I have been thinking the same thing," said Sitric Silkbeard.

A messenger brought Brian Boru an invitation to visit Sitric in Dublin. "Sitric wants to formally present you with the title of overlord of the town," the messenger said.

Brian and Murcha quarreled over it. "You'll be walking into a trap," Murcha warned. "As soon as you enter the gates, Sitric will have you killed."

"I take a lot of killing," Brian replied. "If I refuse to go, my enemies will think I am afraid. The last thing I want is for anyone to think I am fearful."

"Aren't you ever afraid like mortal men?" Murcha burst out.

Brian did not answer.

After Murcha had left Kincora in a temper, Brian thought to himself, I wish I could tell my son that I am afraid, that all men are afraid. That the only weapon we have against our fear is a brave face.

But Murcha is my son. I do not want him to think that I am ever afraid of anything.

Surrounded by a Dalcassian bodyguard, and followed by hundreds of mounted Munstermen and spear carriers on foot, Brian rode east to Dublin. Passing through Leinster he was not challenged. Maelmora stayed behind the walls of his stronghold.

The historian, Carroll, went with Brian on this journey. "Write of it, Carroll," Brian told him.

"Let my name be in the books. I want to be remembered when I am gone."

"When your soul has gone to heavenly glory," said Carroll, who was a pious man.

Brian gave him a sharp look. "Do you think my soul will go to heaven? There is so much blood on my hands."

Carroll was surprised to discover that the great King of Munster was worried about the future of his soul.

The party approached Dublin. Years of warfare had done their damage. Brian and his men passed many a burned, deserted homestead, and many a field crying out with neglect. The Norse of Dublin had raided their Irish neighbors for women and cattle. Both were now rare in the area. Fertile land lay fallow. What a waste, thought Brian. That earth could be supporting Irish and Norse both.

Closer to Dublin they began seeing more people; the town was so crowded they overflowed the walls. The wattle-and-daub huts of the poor straggled out across the countryside. Wealthier classes, traders and craftsmen, lived inside the timber palisade.

As he rode through the gates, Brian curled his nostrils. Dublin smelled terrible. Because of its marshy location, the town had very poor drainage. Brian thought with longing of the sweet, clean wind blowing off Lough Derg.

He and his men had to dismount as soon as they were inside the gates. The town was cramped and crowded, with countless narrow lanes a man must travel on foot. These lanes were lined with stalls where merchants sold their goods. Post-and-wattle fences jealously divided tiny plots of property. Dirty, half-naked children peered from every doorway, reminding Brian that the Norse did not share the Irish custom of bathing. Dublin rang with noise, like the roar of the sea but harsher, more manmade.

And from every quarter came the clink of metal coins.

Brian said over his shoulder to Carroll, "Sitric Silkbeard intends to have coins struck here with his own image on them. The Irish way of using cattle or corn as a medium of exchange is not good enough for him, it seems. He wants clanking money such as they use on the Continent."

Carroll, who was struggling to keep up with Brian as they pushed through the constant crowd, said, "Coins are a good idea. They are more easily carried and exchanged than cattle."

"And more easily stolen," Brian pointed out.

They approached the hall of the Norse king. It was built in the shape of an overturned Viking longship, with a keel for a rooftree and Viking battle standards on poles outside the doorways. "Have them taken down," Brian ordered.

He had to duck his head to pass beneath the lintel of the main doorway. The Norse were tall, but Brian was taller.

Sitric came forward to greet the King of Munster. He had not dressed as a Norse warrior for the occasion, with a bronze helmet and a coat of chain mail. Instead he wore a simple Irish tunic and carried no weapons. He met Brian with a smile and an open hand.

Brian gave back a smile of exactly the same width and warmth, but no more. Sitric was not armed, but his warriors stood all around the walls, and they were armed. I must be very careful here, Brian reminded himself.

Then he saw something that made him forget about being careful.

A woman was standing just beyond Sitric Silkbeard. She was no young girl, but a grown woman, with wise eyes and a proud posture. Her hair was so red its blaze warmed the hall.

Gormla had dressed in her best robes for this occasion. She had been twice a queen: Queen of Dublin as the wife of Olaf Cuaran, and queen again as the wife of the High King of the Irish.

Now she was looking at a man who appeared more kingly than any she had ever seen.

Brian Boru wore a crimson cloak edged with wolf fur, and gold gleamed around his neck and arms and wrists. His huge sword rode at his side in its scabbard. A shortsword with naked blade was thrust through his belt, and he had left the bloodstains on it for all to see. He stalked into the Viking hall like a giant cat, and Gormla drew in her breath sharply.

Sitric had seen the King of Munster before, on

the battlefield at Glenn Mauma. Brian had frightened Sitric badly then, so badly he left the battle and fled back to Dublin. Seeing Brian up close now, Sitric had a desire to flee again. He remembered all too clearly his last sight of Brian Boru, standing amid a heap of Viking corpses and swinging a bloody ax as if he would never tire.

Sitric made himself stand his ground, however. At least Brian was smiling. Then he realized Brian was not smiling at him anymore, but at someone who stood at Sitric's shoulder.

"So this is the Lion of Thomond!" Gormla said in her most charming voice.

Brian Boru spent a seven-night as Sitric's guest in Dublin. Waiting for him, his warriors talked among themselves, wondering what was happening inside the Viking hall.

"King Brian is making the foreigners crawl to him and lick his feet," one Dalcassian claimed.

"Not a bit of it," said another. "He's demanding more plunder for us. If any of Sitric's men refuse, he is clubbing them to the earth with his fists."

A third man said, "Ah, there's no one on the ridge of the world to equal him!"

When at last Brian appeared and said he was ready to return to Munster, he had no more plunder with him. Nor had he clubbed anyone to the earth. His days had been spent talking with Sitric Silkbeard and the Viking princes about trade, and the goods they would be sending to Munster in the future, to the overlord, Brian Boru.

His evenings were spent with the Princess Gormla.

On the journey back to Munster, Brian's men noticed that he was quieter than usual. He had a faraway look in his eyes and did not always hear what was said to him. "The king is tired," they told one another. "He had to match the Vikings drink for drink in their hall, and argue with Sitric night and day."

Brian said nothing.

When he reached Kincora, Ducholi was not waiting to greet him. "She had a bitter argument with Prince Murcha and has gone home to her father in Connacht," her attendants told Brian.

Once he would have sent for her, or gone himself to bring her back. But he did neither. "She has never been really happy here," he said. "Munster ways are not like Connacht ways, and my children did not make Ducholi welcome. I am grateful to her for the help and support she gave me while she was at Kincora, and I hope she will be happier back in Connacht."

Brian's court buzzed with talk. People were surprised by Brian's reaction. He did not even seem to be angry at Murcha for driving Ducholi away.

"But then," as Carroll said to Mac Liag the bard, "Brian Boru is a man full of surprises. Sometimes I myself find him hard to understand."

Brian continued to puzzle his followers. Messengers were sent back and forth between Kincora and Dublin—messengers sworn to secrecy. Everyone had a guess; no one knew for certain. "The king is buying Viking boats to use on the Shannon," someone suggested.

Then Brian left Kincora for Cashel, from which kingly announcements were always made.

At the Fort of the Swords, Malachy could hardly believe his ears when the news reached him. "Say that again. Slowly!" he ordered the messenger. As he listened, he began to laugh. He laughed so hard he gave himself hiccups and had to drink a great deal of wine.

When the High King recovered, he told his companions, "Brian Boru has overstepped himself at last!"

He ordered a feast to be prepared in honor of the announced marriage of the King of Munster.

The High King's confessor was shocked. "How can King Brian marry the Princess Gormla? Does he not already have a wife?"

"He does," said Malachy. "She is Ducholi, the daughter of the King of Connacht. They have had children together, but she has left his roof and now sleeps under her father's roof again. According to the ancient Irish law, this means the marriage is over."

"Not according to Christian law," said the priest sternly.

Malachy was a tolerant man. "The two exist side by side in this land," he said. "Each law serves us well in its turn. The Irish law allowed me to set aside Gormla, and that was a good thing for me altogether. And a bad thing for Brian Boru!'' he added. He began to laugh again, so hard the priest feared for Malachy's health.

"She will destroy him,'' the High King kept saying. "Gormla will destroy Brian without my having to lift a finger! She will turn his beard gray and have him talking to himself before the year is out.''

Malachy had not been so cheerful for years.

The priests of Munster, including Brian's brother, the abbot Marcan, did not openly criticize this new marriage. Brian had been very generous to the Church. He had rebuilt many churches and abbeys and endowed more. No man could claim Brian Boru did not serve God well.

Nor did anyone speak openly about the traditional offerings he still took to the spirit who watched from the gray crag.

Even Murcha did not complain about Brian's marrying Gormla. He said to his wife, "I expected my father to blame me for Ducholi's desertion. He has not done so, and now I know why. He is always making plans in his head, and this Gormla is part of his latest plan. Marrying her will give him an alliance with Leinster, as well as with Dublin. This is just another move in the game he plays, I see it now. It does not mean he loves the woman. He loved only my mother,'' Murcha insisted. He had convinced himself of this now. As a result, he found it easier to be with Brian, and so in time he came to Kincora, met the newest wife, and was even pleasant to her.

Gormla liked Kincora. From the beginning, however, she had suggestions for making it better. "You should have fourteen doorways in your feasting hall, like the feasting hall at Tara," she told Brian.

"What makes you think I want to copy Tara?"

Gormla laughed. "Ah, Brian, I know you better than you know yourself. We are very much alike. I don't think you want to copy Tara. I think you want Tara."

He did not argue with her.

Gormla was a very different sort of woman from Brian's other wives, gentle Mor and merry Achra and elegant Ducholi. Gormla had a restless mind that was always planning and scheming.

Like Brian's own.

At first Brian enjoyed her. But as the days passed and she continued to make suggestions that were sounding more and more like demands, he began to ignore her.

"Gormla has a great opinion of herself," he told Mac Liag. "She thinks every idea she has is a pearl. But she is already with child, I am happy to say. That will fill her thoughts soon enough and she will stop hanging over my shoulder."

Mac Liag, who had been watching the Leinster-woman, was not certain even motherhood would change her as Brian expected.

Even when she was large with child Gormla always managed to be on hand when a messenger arrived with news from the world beyond Kincora. She had very definite ideas about how Brian should enlarge his rule, and she did not hesitate to tell him. Continually.

"My son Sitric is unmarried," she said. "And you have a daughter just reaching the age for marriage. Such a tie would bind Sitric and his Norsemen more surely to you."

For once, Brian agreed with Gormla's suggestion. He asked his daughter Emer to come to him in a small private chamber where they could talk. Emer was a daughter of his second wife, Achra, and was a girl of spirit and laughter. Of all his daughters, she was the one closest to her father.

Brian patted the bench beside him, inviting Emer to sit on the carved oak seat with its down-filled cushion. At first he spoke of homely things— "How is your embroidery? Do you like the caged larks I gave you?"

Then he slowly brought the talk around to the subject at hand.

"When Vikings have visited me here at Kincora, you have admired them," he reminded Emer.

"Many of them are good to look upon," the girl replied.

"Have you thought of marrying one?"

Emer blushed.

"If a daughter of mine were married to a Viking," Brian went on, "it would show everyone that I mean to bring Irish and foreigner together as one people.''

''Is there one particular Viking you have in mind?'' Emer wanted to know.

''Sitric, King of Dublin, is young and strong, a man-sized man who owns many ships.''

''Gormla's son?''

''The same.''

Emer considered this. ''Would it please you, Father, if I married Sitric?''

Brian smiled fondly at his favorite daughter. ''It would please me if you want to marry him after you've met him. I would never ask otherwise.''

Emer blushed again. In a low voice, she said, ''Then invite him to Kincora, Father.''

Gormla was delighted. ''What a good team we make!'' she told Brian. ''Admit it, you would not have thought of such a thing without me. But it is good for all concerned.''

Brian had to agree. The next day he said to Mac Liag, ''I was clever to marry a clever woman.''

Emer waited eagerly for Sitric Silkbeard. She was prepared to accept him even before she saw him. In asking her to consider the match, Brian had been asking for Emer's help. She loved her father with all her heart. What other maiden had such a father? She had never been able to do anything to help him, he was always so busy, striding here, galloping there, meeting with his princes, issuing orders. He was like a comet flashing by.

Now at last he needed her.

And fortunately, Sitric when he arrived was indeed good to look upon.

When the proposed marriage was announced, Murcha came at the gallop. "This is another mistake," he said to Brian. "We recently fought Sitric. Why marry your daughter to him? He is your enemy."

"That's the very point, Murcha. I am trying to change things so he won't always be my enemy. Emer will bear his children and turn foreigners into Irishmen."

Aware of Brian's political moves, Malachy began to feel the hot breath of the King of Munster on his own neck. He had no doubt that Brian would challenge him for the high kingship soon. So he summoned all his allies to a great meeting at Tara.

Malachy was disappointed at how few men came. Most of them were Meathmen. The northern O'Neills sent a token party only. According to tradition, when Malachy was no longer High King his place would be taken by one of the northern O'Neills. They were merely waiting for him to die.

Waiting for Brian Boru to kill me, Malachy thought bitterly. But the O'Neills will never let him seize the high kingship. Never!

Then Brian Boru marched an enormous army out of Munster, northward. In advance of this movement, Brian's new son-in-law, Sitric Silkbeard, had made a raid by river and sea into Ulster with Brian's lion banners fluttering from the prows of his ships.

The message was not wasted on the O'Neill princes in the north. The King of Munster was now allied with Dublin. That meant he had the strength of the Norsemen behind him. He also had the support of Connacht still, and he had demanded and received warriors from Maelmora of Leinster.

As Brian told his historian, Carroll, "When the time comes for me to challenge Malachy for the high kingship, I must know if his O'Neill kinsmen will support him."

"Are you prepared to fight the princes of Ulster?"

"I hope I won't have to," Brian replied. "If I have planned wisely, and the size of my army makes them timid, I may win without shedding a drop of blood."

"This is a strange sort of warfare altogether!" Carroll said.

Brian laughed. "Many of the things I do seem strange to other people."

"That's because you think in new ways," the historian told him.

"I wish my son Murcha understood that."

"Ah, Brian, I think he does. He just won't admit it. He's as proud as you are."

Brian's army flowed across the land. Considering that their leader wanted to avoid bloodshed, they were heavily armed indeed. In addition to the usual foot warriors, Brian had a cavalry comprising both Irish riders and Norsemen from Dublin, mounted on sturdy ponies.

The army advanced on Ulster. People all along the way came out of their forts and farms to see them pass. Points of light glittered on the polished weapons and in the eyes of the warriors. There was no singing along the way. These men were veterans of battle and the singing had gone out of them.

Meanwhile, Malachy was sending frantic messages to his northern kinsmen, asking their support against Brian. But as Brian moved deeper into Ulster, the princes of the north observed the size of his army and delayed sending a reply of any sort to Malachy.

Brian marched on. He never attacked, he never declared war on any person. He merely marched, and his army followed.

The princes of Ulster stayed quiet behind barred doors. Not one of them could command as many warriors as Brian Boru.

At last one, the Prince Hugh, felt he must face the Dalcassian. According to tradition, Hugh should follow Malachy as High King.

Gathering his followers and the warriors sworn to him, Hugh went to meet Brian at Dundalk. With him were a number of the Ulster princes. There was the usual argument among them as to who should formally greet the King of Munster.

Brian's army waited like a dark mantle spread across the land. Finally Hugh himself came forward, fully armed and looking tense.

When they met, Brian said, "I call the blessings of God upon the tribe O'Neill."

Hugh was caught unprepared. "You are not here to attack?"

"Attack?" Brian asked as if he did not know the meaning of the word. He seemed unaware of the huge army at his back, though Hugh kept looking at it.

"You invade Ulster with an army," Hugh accused.

Now Brian glanced around, then looked back at Hugh and grinned. "You mean my followers? They are merely good people who have made this journey with me because they want to see more of the land than just Munster. We have not harmed a person we met along our way."

Hugh was not reassured. "The High King sends word to us that you are threatening him."

Brian grinned even more. "You just said I brought an army to Ulster. So how can I be threatening Meath? I assure you I don't have two armies. The men you see with me are all I have."

The men with him were quite enough, Hugh thought.

Hugh was not a reckless man. Nor was he a young one. If there was going to be a struggle for the high kingship, he decided he was too old to get involved. The one time he had visited Tara he had thought the place shabby and in need of much repair. No High King had made it his residence for a very long time. Now it was used only for ceremonial occasions, as Brian used Cashel. Tara's timbered halls were rotting, and a constant wind blew across the green ridge and through holes in its roofs. A wind like a banshee's cry.

"If you intend no harm you're welcome," Hugh said to Brian.

"I intend the opposite of harm. I want to right a wrong. I understand that some raiders from Dublin, flying my standard, recently pillaged your lands?"

"They did."

"Then rather than taking cattle, women, and hostages from you, will you allow me to offer you a gift to make up for what was taken?" As he spoke, Brian gave a signal and some of his men trotted forward, carrying great chests filled with treasure. They set these at the feet of the astonished Hugh.

"I would not have the noble O'Neills suffer any loss in the name of Brian Boru," the King of Munster said.

Hugh looked past Brian one more time, at the huge army with him. An army large enough to take anything in sight, if it wanted.

If Brian Boru wanted.

Hugh was a wise man. "The O'Neills of the north have no quarrel with Brian of Munster," he announced at last.

Brian spent three days with the northern princes. They served great feasts in his honor, and his bards taught their bards the poetry of the south.

"And that's how you win a war without bloodshed,'' Brian told Carroll when they were on their way back to Munster.

When they reached Kincora, they found that a small war had broken out there. Gormla had been bored with Brian away. She had managed to start a fight among some of the Dalcassians left to guard his stronghold. Brian arrived just in time to put a stop to it before someone was killed.

The quarrel was forgotten when the annual tribute from the Limerick Danes arrived. Every year since their defeat at his hands they had sent him 365 tuns of wine containing 32 gallons each. This was kept in the wine cellar Brian had built across the Shannon, out of easy reach of his warriors. But to make his Dalcassians put aside their differences he ordered the wine to flow like water at Kincora, until no man remembered what the fight was about.

Brian did not take part. He climbed alone to the gray crag. There he whispered, to the listening spirit of Aval, ''When I married her, I thought Gormla would make me happy. She was not like any of my other women. I could talk to her and she understood. I thought she would be a companion as we grew older.

''Perhaps I made a mistake, Aval.''

He looked out across the land, across Lough Derg and the shimmering Shannon and the walls of Kincora.

''Perhaps the only thing that it is safe to love is the land itself,'' Brian said sadly.

The land could not die. The land never disappointed him.

He stretched out his arms in love and longing, as if he would embrace all of Ireland.

THIRTEEN

Marching on Tara

M arcan mac Kennedy was pleased with the abbey his brother Brian had ordered built for him. As its abbot he had reached the limit of his worldly ambition. He also enjoyed knowing the abbey was safe from raiders. In the land Brian Boru controlled, raids on abbeys and monasteries had all but ceased. When anyone sought to plunder them, Brian hunted down the thieves and punished them savagely.

If Brian was trying to bring peace to Ireland, it seemed he was also trying to make his own peace with God.

But peace was not as easily won as a battle. In the province of Connacht, King Conor decided his daughter Ducholi had been insulted by Brian. ''But

I don't want to live with him anymore, Father," she insisted, but Conor would not listen. He rebelled against Brian and declared support for Malachy instead.

Brian was forced to march into Connacht and put down the rising. Irish blood was shed by Irishmen, and Brian felt it on his hands.

How long could he hope to hold his allies together, he wondered? Irish and Viking were an uneasy partnership at best. He did not believe Sitric and Maelmora would be loyal to him just for the sake of Gormla. She was using her influence on his behalf now, but that could change. One could never predict what Gormla might do.

Brian sent for Mac Liag. They sat together drinking red wine in a stone chamber lined with hangings of brightly dyed wool. A fire burned in a bronze brazier near their feet, to keep away the chill that lingered in spite of the springtime. One of Brian's beloved shaggy hounds was stretched beside the king's bench. The dog appeared to be asleep, but when Brian spoke it opened its eyes and thumped its tail against the stone floor.

"Malachy will probably never again feel as weak as he does now," Brian said. "I know he isn't afraid of me. I have simply outsmarted him. If I am ever to challenge him, this is the time. And I should like Donncha, the son Gormla has given me, to grow up as the son of a High King.

"I shall ask Marcan my brother to come from his abbey and bless me, Mac Liag. Then I shall lead an army into Meath and demand Malachy submit to me.''

For a long time, Mac Liag had expected to hear those words. For a long time, Brian had made no secret of his ambition.

"Take me with you, Brian," said Mac Liag. "I want to see it happen with my own eyes, so I can compose a great poem about it afterward."

"You and Carroll will both go with me," Brian promised.

Murcha was going, too. On such an occasion, Brian could not leave his oldest son behind. Even knowing there might be trouble between them—for when was there not?—Brian asked Murcha to ride at his shoulder.

All the years of planning and dreaming were coming together now. If Brian succeeded and Malachy surrendered the high kingship to him, he meant to rule a newly united Ireland, a thing that had never been before. And he wanted Murcha to be part of it, to understand, and to follow him when he was gone and hold together what Brian had built.

Irish and Viking together at peace. Peace among the tribes. A land where no child would find its mother slaughtered.

In the early summer of the Year of Our Lord 1002, Brian Boru marched into Meath. The lion banner was vivid in the sunlight.

Brian sent a messenger ahead to Malachy, demanding that he surrender Tara and the high kingship.

The army advanced very slowly. Brian wanted to give the High King time to accept his fate and submit without fighting. Once again, the people watched as Brian Boru passed by. Some among them noticed that he wore a cloak of seven colors. Only the High King was entitled to wear seven colors.

When he learned that Brian was approaching with an army, Malachy sent one last, desperate appeal north, to Ulster.

The reply came back. "If you want us to stand with you against Munster," Hugh O'Neill said, "you must give us half of Meath."

Malachy could not give up his homeland. Feeling totally deserted, he waited alone, except for his little band of loyal Meath princes, in the echoing halls of Tara.

At last runners came to tell him Brian and his army were setting up camp on the plains beyond. Malachy felt a curious sense of relief. At least the long wait was over. "How large is the army?" he asked.

"They blacken the earth, and the smoke from their fires blackens the sky."

"Ah," said Malachy. "Ah."

Twilight fell on royal Meath. By himself, wishing no company, Malachy wandered through the deserted halls of Tara, murmuring their names to himself. The Fort of the Kings. The Fort of the Synods. King Laoire's Fort. The great feasting hall with its fourteen doorways, where he had celebrated in times past. Empty now, the chieftains who had cheered him gone. Their banners hung limp and forgotten in the damp evening air.

Malachy wondered what Kincora was like. Larger than Tara, some said. Grander than the Fort of the Swords.

"I have been a good king," Malachy said aloud, as if challenging the night wind to answer him.

He walked a little farther. A stone glinted white in the fading light. Drawing back his foot, Malachy gave it a kick, then listened to it rattle away in the darkness.

"What did I do wrong?" he asked aloud.

The night wind had no answer for him.

At dawn, a sleepless and red-eyed Malachy put on his finest robes and prepared to meet Brian Boru.

FOURTEEN

Brian Claims the High Kingship

With Tara rising behind him, Malachy approached Brian across Mag Breg, the Plain of Hills. He came as a High King should, accompanied by his standard bearer and most loyal princes, and followed by a guard of honor composed of his best warriors with their swords.

The warriors carried the swords outstretched, in surrender.

This was the moment Brian had waited for, for so long. He wanted to stop time, so he could enjoy it. But it would rush past and be over; even he could not stop time. His bard and historian must capture the moment for him.

As he watched Malachy approach his tent, Brian issued an order. "Collect as many of our best horses as Malachy has warriors with him.''

When the High King was twelve paces away, Brian stepped forward six paces, halving the distance.

Their warriors formed a circle around them, jostling one another in their eagerness to be in front and see and hear all that was said.

Whatever Brian might take from him, Malachy was a prince of the O'Neills, a man of dignity and personal courage. He held his head high and met Brian's eyes with a steady gaze of his own. ''If those who should have supported me had not failed me, I would meet you with raised shields between us, Brian Boru.''

In a deep voice Brian replied, ''I am willing to meet you in single combat anytime, Malachy.''

The High King sighed. ''It would serve no purpose. The contest between us is already over, and we both know it.''

Raising his arms, he lifted a circlet of gold from his head. ''I have worn this for twenty years,'' he said to Brian. ''See if it fits you.''

Brian took the crown of the High King. Gazing down at it, he turned it over and over in his fingers. The men watched eagerly but his face told them nothing of the thoughts behind his eyes.

This is only metal, he was saying to himself. Like the title, *High King,* it means nothing by itself. Whatever meaning it has, men give it.

He looked up and gave Malachy a gentle smile. ''You are a noble man,'' he said. Then, to the astonishment of all, he put his arms around the smaller Meathman and embraced him. As they broke apart Brian put the crown back into Malachy's hands.

"This isn't mine until I am made High King in the ancient ritual," he said. "Until then, it should remain with you. And I should also like to give you the sort of gift kings of equal rank exchange." He turned and beckoned. Horseboys ran forward, leading the best Munster horses, one for every member of Malachy's party.

The High King's own men cheered Brian Boru.

Now that it was too late, Malachy began to realize what he had done wrong. He had followed all the traditions. As High King, he had demanded taxes in the form of tributes, taken sides in tribal feuds, fought and feasted and enjoyed the wealth of his rank. He had done what all the High Kings before him had done.

But Brian Boru had a different idea of kingship. He won support and admiration through gestures such as this, without fighting. He had made himself the image of what a High King should be.

Nobility comes more naturally to him than it does to me, Malachy thought sadly, though I was born to a great tribe and he an unimportant one. It was my misfortune to be born in the same generation as such a man.

Malachy ordered the feasting hall of Tara swept and garnished once again, so he could serve a feast in honor of the Lion of Thomond. He shall at least see me lose gracefully, Malachy promised himself. One last feast in the ancient hall, while the crown is still on my head.

"I assume that Prince Murcha will be his father's Tanist, the man chosen to succeed him," Malachy told his servants. "I have heard that Brian has been trying to train his oldest son for that purpose. So seat him at his father's side for the feast."

Sitting beside Brian, Murcha watched him closely. Other men at the feast were eating right-and-left-handed and emptying their wine cups as fast as they were filled. Brian ate well, but drank very little. He sat quiet and watchful, always in control of himself.

When a servant approached with more wine, Murcha put his hand over his cup as Brian did. I can learn from you, Father, he thought to himself. He saw Brian's glance flick toward him, noticing. Then Brian gave the smallest nod of approval, one that none but Murcha saw.

Murcha smiled.

My son seems to have learned something from my bloodless victory, Brian thought. He is looking at me with new respect in his eyes. I suppose he never really expected me to become High King.

Nor did I! Brian suddenly admitted to himself. He felt joy swelling his chest. Joy, and a growing sense of the huge responsibility he was about to take upon himself.

At the doorways of the feasting hall, the banners of the chieftains hung from their poles. For the first

time a banner of yellow silk hung among them—
yellow silk, upon which were three crimson lions.

Brian did not send for Gormla to join him when
he was formally made High King. Gormla had
been Malachy's wife. He would not use her as salt
to rub in the other man's wound.

At Kincora, she complained bitterly about being
left out.

Brian's army remained encamped on the plain
below Tara while preparations were made for the
ceremony. It was best to be prepared. No one could
say how the tribes of Ireland might react to this
break with tradition. The overthrow of a High King
could shake the very earth upon which they stood,
even if it was done without blood.

Each of the five great roads leading to Tara was
guarded by a company of armed Dalcassians.

On the appointed day, a huge crowd came up
those roads to see Brian become High King. Farmers had left their fields, women had left their pots
boiling over the fire, children had left their play.
Everyone wanted to be at Tara. An excited buzz ran
through the crowd. "The Stone of Fal is supposed
to cry out when a true king is crowned. Will it cry
out for the Dalcassian, do you suppose?"

No one knew.

As historian of the south, Carroll had argued that
Brian should be crowned at Cashel. But Brian had
replied, "I am already King of Munster. The Stone
of Fal at Tara is the sacred symbol of high king-

ship. I shall claim Ireland from the Stone of Fal or not at all.''

Hearing these words, Brian's men had exchanged worried looks. Everyone knew the legend about the Stone of Fal, but most thought it was only a legend. Had the stone cried out for Malachy? Had he even bothered to stand upon it, according to the ancient tradition?

Brian sent for his brother, the abbot Marcan, to place the gold circlet upon his head when the time came. When Brian mentioned the Stone of Fal, Marcan said, ''The voice in the stone is the voice of a demon, brother! It cried out for pagan kings. A Christian should have nothing to do with such a symbol.''

Brian gave Marcan a long look. ''This land was pagan before it was Christian. This land is many things. You cannot cut out the parts you don't like and throw them away, any more than I could drive out the Vikings.''

Of all of Brian's followers, Murcha was the most worried. ''What if my father steps onto the stone and it makes no sound?'' he kept asking Mac Liag. ''What sort of poem will you compose then?''

FIFTEEN

Emperor of the Irish

B rian knew how important symbols were. He had made much use of symbols in his career. The strong walls of Kincora, the generosity of his gifts, the size of his army. These were symbols everyone understood. The Stone of Fal was the greatest symbol of all.

On the day before the ceremony, Brian went to see Tara for himself. No kings lived there now, but it was the true heart of the land as it had been since the days of the Tuatha de Danann.

"I am here at last, Aval," Brian whispered to the wind. "On my own terms."

He stopped before the Stone of Fal. The bards said the stone had been brought to Ireland by the Dananns in ancient times, before the coming of the

Gael. The Gael had fought and defeated the Dananns, but kept their magical stone to crown their own kings upon. As a little boy, Brian had never tired of hearing the tales of conquests and heroic deeds.

So many conquests, he thought. Let it be over now.

The surface of the gray stone was rough and pitted. It lay flat on the earth, atop the Mound of the Hostages, as the sacred oak of the Dalcassians had stood on its mound at Magh Adhair before Malachy cut it down. There were two shallow hollows in the stone like the prints of forgotten feet. These marked where a king should stand—if he dared.

Brian walked slowly around the stone, his eyes narrowed in thought.

Tomorrow the Stone of Fal must cry aloud. It must announce him as the true and rightful High King.

Nothing must be left to chance, he told himself.

At dawn the next morning, Marcan came for him. Brian had dressed with care for the most important occasion of his life. His mane of red-gold hair was fading at last, and streaked with gray, but its damp waves bore the toothmarks of his comb. His head was bare, awaiting a crown.

He wore a new tunic with bell-shaped, pleated sleeves, and Celtic knotwork around the hem. It was belted with fine Munster leather, ornamented with gold. But the belt held no scabbard. For the first time in many years, Brian Boru carried no weapons.

His standard bearer came forward, lifting the banner of three crimson lions. The king and his party followed it up the hill. They were soon surrounded by the crowd of people who had come from as far away as Dublin to see the event. The air was filled with the voices of trumpets.

When Brian entered the main gate of Tara, a hush fell over the crowd. Malachy was waiting near the Stone of Fal. Malachy had not used the stone during his own inauguration ceremony. His priests had been against the pagan custom. Now Malachy could not help noticing the way the people looked at the stone, with fear and something like reverence. Pagan and Christian lived side by side in these people.

The ceremony began with a reading from the Book of Rights, describing the duties of kingship. These laws had come to Ireland with the Gael, fifteen hundred years before Brian was born. When he swore to uphold them, the people nodded approval.

"He looks like one of the kings from the ancient stories," they said to one another.

Next the historian recited Brian's family history, so all present would know he was of noble blood. Finally, Marcan turned to Malachy and held out his hands.

Malachy had tried to prepare himself for this moment. But when he lifted the gold circlet from his own head and handed it to the Dalcassian abbot, he felt an awful sense of loss.

Marcan carried the circlet to Brian. As chief poet to the king, Mac Liag would hand Brian the white rod of authority, another pagan symbol. Marcan would set the High King's crown on Brian's head and recite a Christian blessing. The old and the new were mingled in the ceremony.

Irish and Viking were mingled in the audience, watching. Among them stood the leading clerics of the area, bishops and abbots from Kells and Clonard, Durrow and Finglas. Brian had given gifts to all their churches.

An ancient wind sang through the halls of Tara.

With the rod of polished hazelwood in one hand and the gold circlet on his brow, Brian stepped on to the Stone of Fal.

For many years afterward, people would ask each other, ''Were you on Tara Hill when the Stone of Fal cried aloud for Brian Boru?''

Even those who had not been there would claim, later, that they had. Even those who had not heard the stone would try, later, to describe its sound for others. The sound was not to be forgotten. It was a chilling wail that rose like the shriek of a banshee and arched across Ireland like a rainbow, uniting the Hill of Tara with the Gray Crag of Thomond.

Afterward, Brian returned to Kincora. It was time to start putting into effect the years of plans he had stored in his head. There were so many things he wanted to do for the land he loved; the land that could not die like a mother, or disappoint like a son, or be carried away like gold.

Brian built churches and schools and bridges. When men broke the law, he dealt justice with such a firm hand that violence all but disappeared from the land. When tribal quarrels broke out, Brian was tireless in settling them.

Step by step, day by day, he enforced his will on the people as no High King before him had ever attempted to do.

And step by step, day by day, a new serenity extended over the island of Ireland.

Mac Liag wrote with delight of a time when a fair maiden, dressed in all her finery and jewels, could travel the length of the land without meeting theft or insult in any form.

"Let no man forget," Brian told the historians and scribes, "that I have a strong hand. I am not afraid to give out punishment, as three thousand Danes learned on Singland Hill after the battle of Sulcoit. They used violence against my people and I met them with a greater violence. Let that be a warning."

Brian did not want anyone to forget that he could be savage. The war-loving princes of the tribes must know that his strong hand was uppermost.

Brian was sixty-one years of age when he became High King, but as his giant shadow stretched across the land, people did not think of him as old. He was Ireland's strength and her pride.

With peace came growth. More children lived to

grow up. Seedlings were planted to replace the timber the Vikings had taken for their ships. Even the weather seemed milder, so that spring lasted for half a year and fine crops were harvested.

"I intend to involve myself in things Malachy never thought about," Brian told Murcha. He made a tour of the entire island, talking to its people, examining its coastline, planning how it should be defended if invaders ever came again. These plans he told to Murcha, to remember and use if they should ever be needed. "Pass them on to your son," Brian said.

He also visited Armagh, in the north, where he left a gift of twenty ounces of gold on the altar and declared Armagh to be the primary ecclesiastical city in Ireland.

The bishops were highly pleased. They offered a vellum book for his inscription, to be added to the Annals of Armagh.

"You have won the hearts of the Ulstermen," they assured Brian.

"They may speak for God," the High King said quietly to Carroll, who was with his party. "But I doubt if they speak for all of the O'Neills. Still, it is no small thing to have won the support of the Church in the north. Fetch your inks and quills, Carroll, and let us attend to this page."

When the vellum page was returned to the bishops they read, in a beautifully clear and trained hand, the words:

"St. Patrick, when going to heaven, decreed that

the entire fruit of his labor, as well of baptism and causes as of alms, should be rendered to the apostolic city, which in the Irish tongue is called Ard Macha. Thus I have found it in the records of the Irish. Thus I have written, in the presence of Brian, Emperor of the Irish.''

Emperor of the Irish. The bishops clustered around to read the words.

Written by Maelsuthainn mac Carroll, those words on that page survive until this very day, and may be read still in the Book of Armagh.

Brian made many other journeys. His relentless energy had not deserted him. He accepted the submissions of chieftains who had hardly heard his name before he appeared in their gateways with an army at his back. There was little fighting done, however. Usually the sight of Brian's strength was enough.

Peace spread and multiplied. Children slept safely in their beds.

But there was not much peace at Kincora. Gormla had never forgiven Brian for not taking her to Tara, to share his glory. She had wanted to throw her triumph in Malachy's face. Her disappointment made her curdle like milk left in the sun.

When Brian was with her she gave him the sharp edge of her tongue. He was more patient with her than he should be, some said.

''If my wife spoke to me like that I would pluck her like a chicken,'' said Brian's confessor, who was a gentle priest with a fine Christian spirit and a devoted wife and children. Priests in Rome did not marry, but Irish priests had not accepted that custom. They considered families sacred.

Brian had laughed at the priest's words. "What Gormla says can't hurt me. People have said much worse things about me."

Murcha pointed out, "It isn't what she says, Father. It's what she may do. She might try to turn her brother and even her son against you."

Murcha did not like young Donncha, son of Brian and Gormla.

But Brian ignored the warning. Murcha has not liked any of my women, he told himself. I can handle Gormla.

SIXTEEN

Trouble Brewing

Brian never lied to himself. Sometimes he had to admit to himself what he would admit to no one else—he was getting old. In wet weather his knees and shoulders ached all the time, and there were mornings when it was very hard indeed to get up and face the day.

All his life he had thought about so many things, but never about being old. Age had crept up on him while he was busy elsewhere. His body was not the body he knew, but he was trapped in it. Trapped in flesh from which the strength was fading.

Once he awoke in the middle of the night, shaking as if he had a chill. "What's wrong?" Gormla asked, but he would not tell her.

Brian did not want to be old. He remembered

when he was young and strong. He remembered when he was a little boy, the youngest of a large family, running and laughing and playing rowdy games from morning till night.

That was all behind him now. The friends, the fun, the freedom of childhood. Now he was Brian Boru. And in the darkness of the night, even with Gormla beside him, he was alone.

In the not-too-distant future, he would die. Who would care about and protect the land as he did?

In the great hall of Kincora, as they sat together over their wine, Brian said to his chief poet, "If I asked you to compose a poem about the bravest of my sons, who would you name, Mac Liag?"

"All your sons are brave. But that honor would have to go to the oldest, Prince Murcha."

"And if I asked you to name the wisest of my sons, who would you name then?"

Mac Liag considered for a long time before answering. "Prince Murcha was the best at his studies."

"Being clever is not the same as being wise. Soon I must formally announce the name of my Tanist, the man I choose to succeed me. When I am gone, will my kingdom be safe in the hands of Murcha?"

"Ah." Mac Liag gazed at the flames. He took longer still before he said, "You are a strong man with many years left in you, Brian. By the time you are no longer able to be High King, Murcha will have grown wiser. He will be the best man in the land to follow you. There is much of you in him, more than in any of the others.''

Brian nodded, satisfied. ''And Murcha's son Turlough contains much of his father. We are a dynasty, Mac Liag. Father to son.''

''A dynasty must have a history,'' Brian said the next day to Carroll. ''I shall send out a summons, asking the historians of all the major tribes to come to me at Cashel. They are to write a new book, giving the history of this land from its earliest times. Attention is to be paid to the noble bloodlines of the Dalcassians—particular attention, Carroll.''

The book Brian wanted was prepared. Included in it were his ideas of kingship and justice. The best from both the Brehon law and Christian teaching were worked into the text. The book was to be known as the Psalter of Cashel. ''And,'' Brian announced, ''it is to include a record of my defeats as well as my victories, so no man can claim this history is false.''

Taking Carroll aside, he then said to the chief historian, ''Just be certain the book is worded so the victories far outnumber the defeats. There are ways of making victories seem more glorious than they were, and defeats less shameful.

''And whatever you do, Carroll, give no insult to my enemies. A true king honors a beaten foe.''

Carroll understood. Brian Boru, who was far from perfect, wanted future generations to think of him as perfect.

Who could blame him? He was Ireland's strength and pride.

When Murcha was named as Brian's Tanist, Gormla and her son, Donncha, were both angry. Donncha was jealous of his half-brothers. Six of them had actually fought in battles under the leadership of their father. Donncha had yet to fight his first battle.

"It's not fair to choose Murcha over me without knowing what a warrior I will be," he complained to his mother.

"It's not fair to choose Murcha at all," Gormla told Brian. "My son contains more royal blood. Murcha's mother was only the daughter of a tribal king. I am a princess of Leinster."

"I've made my decision," Brian replied. "I am the High King."

"High Kings can be made and unmade," Gormla said under her breath. "Haven't I seen that in my own lifetime?"

Brian's eyes narrowed dangerously. "What did you say? Are you threatening me?"

She wanted to defy him. She had never backed down from any man. But there was a force in Brian that made her drop her eyes and say, "Of course I'm not threatening you. You are the High King."

"Remember that. And remember also, when I am gone, Mor's son Murcha will be High King after me."

He strode from the chamber. Gormla stared after him, clenching her fists. How dare he! she thought.

How dare he choose that dead woman's son over mine!

She stalked through Kincora, complaining about everyone and everything.

"I wish I could put her to work building bridges," Brian remarked to Mac Liag. "Gormla's problem is that she has nothing to do."

"She should have another child to keep her busy."

Brian shook his head. "Donncha was born when she was past the age of childbearing. Another infant would be a miracle. I don't perform miracles."

Mac Liag laughed. "Half of Ireland swears you do. We've had ten years of peace."

Brian did not join in his friend's laughter. "Last night I heard the banshee cry out from the gray crag. The days of peace may be coming to an end."

Mac Liag shuddered.

To give Gormla something to do, Brian decided to invite her brother Maelmora to visit her at Kincora. It was the season when Leinster always sent its tribute to Brian anyway, so Maelmora might as well bring it.

"I have another reason, of course," he said to Murcha.

"Don't you always?"

"Recently I've heard that the King of Leinster is growing restless under my rule. It would be wise to have him see the size of my stronghold, and count the number of warriors I keep here at all times."

"Three thousand now," said Murcha.

"Just so. That should remind the King of Leinster that it is better to obey me than defy me."

Brian told Gormla, "I have to go to Dublin for a time. I keep hearing rumors of possible trouble, and I want to sit down with Sitric Silkbeard and discuss his loyalty. My daughter Emer tells me he talks too much about the old ways, the days of plundering.

"While I am gone, the Leinstermen will be bringing the cattle tribute to Kincora. I have invited your brother to come with them and keep you company."

Gormla scowled. "Maelmora, here? You know that we don't get along well together."

"Make an effort, Gormla. For my sake."

"Who will be in charge here while you're away?"

"Murcha, of course."

Gormla's eyes blazed. "Why not me?"

Brian merely laughed. This made Gormla angrier than ever. She did not go to the gate to see him ride off toward Dublin.

She was there, however, to greet Maelmora when he arrived. She wanted to begin complaining about Brian right away.

Maelmora was in no mood to listen. He resented being summoned by the High King, and the journey had not been a pleasant one. Rain and mud had slowed their progress. As a gift for Brian, Maelmora had brought a selection of timber to be used as masts for Brian's ships. When mud made it difficult for his men to carry the timber, Maelmora had tried to help—and got his clothes torn for his pains.

To silence the stream of Gormla's complaints, he took off the tunic he was wearing and tossed it to her.

"Here, mend this. A silver button was torn from it. Sew it back on for me," he said when they entered the hall.

Gormla's temper exploded. "I'm not your servant! Do your own sewing, you weakling!"

"What do you mean, weakling?"

"Only a weakling would have given in to Brian's demands for such a huge tribute. All those cattle—you should have refused, as I refuse to serve you!" She turned and threw her brother's tunic into the nearest fire.

The smell of burning cloth floated out over Kincora.

Maelmora turned his back on his sister and stalked in a rage into the courtyard.

The courtyard beyond the great hall was paved with flagstones, and surrounded by high walls against which fruit trees were trained. Servants hurried to and fro. The sound of a harp came from some inner chamber. Horses neighed in the stables. Beyond the courtyard, Kincora sprawled in every direction, composed of chambers and halls and lodges and workshops. Busy and prosperous.

The home of the High King.

Everywhere Maelmora looked, he saw some token of Brian's success. Jealousy mixed with anger in the King of Leinster. He was a prince of his tribe, however, and he knew better than to insult Brian's hospitality by leaving on the same day he arrived. So he gritted his teeth and went back into the great hall, determined to put the best face he could on the occasion.

That night an icy rain fell. To pass the time, Murcha and his cousin Conaing, one of Brian's nephews, were playing a game of chess in the great hall. To avoid having to talk to his sister, Maelmora strolled over to watch them. At one stage he thought he saw an opening and said to Murcha, "Move that piece there."

Murcha followed the suggestion. Conaing let out a shout of triumph, made a move of his own, and won the game. Murcha looked up and met Maelmora's eyes. "I seem to remember that you gave Sitric and his Norsemen advice at the battle of Glenn Mauma," he said angrily. "They lost, too. After this, keep your advice to yourself, Maelmora, since you don't know how to win."

Maelmora was glad of the excuse to lose his own temper. "Next time I give your enemies advice, they will win!"

Murcha leaped to his feet, turning over his stool. "In that case, you'd better find another yew tree to hide in, Leinsterman."

Maelmora ground his teeth in fury. At that moment, Gormla laughed. From the shadows at the far end of the hall she had overheard everything. Her contempt poured down on her brother, more brutal than the rain. "You are a cowardly wretch!" she shouted at Maelmora.

He ran from the hall.

When Brian returned from Dublin, Murcha, embarrassed, met him at the main gate. "I let matters get out of hand," he admitted.

"What happened?"

Murcha told Brian in as few words as possible. He finished by saying, "We sent a messenger after Maelmora, asking him to come back, but the King of Leinster and his men fell upon the poor man and left him at the side of the road with a broken skull."

Peace lay shattered like the chessmen on the flagstones at Kincora.

Brian blamed Murcha. "This is your fault. I thought I could leave you in charge, trusting you to act as I would. Now I see that you're not ready to take my place."

"Maelmora lost his temper first. He was spoiling for a fight—so I gave it to him."

"That's no excuse. You did not behave with wisdom and dignity as a king must."

At Brian's elbow, Gormla said, "Punish Murcha. Replace him with my son as your Tanist."

Brian whirled on her. "You aren't without blame in this! Can't I turn my back on any of you? You knew it was important to keep the loyalty of Leinster, but you did everything you could to anger Maelmora. You are forever stirring up trouble. I can't afford it anymore. Pack your things and follow your brother.''

She stared at him in disbelief. ''You're throwing me out? I'm the mother of your son!''

''I have a number of sons,'' Brian told her, ''and one woman too many. Go.''

She dared not argue. In his face she saw something more frightening than anger. She had broken the peace that meant everything to him; he wanted to kill her.

Gormla ran to her chamber and ordered her attendants to begin packing her belongings.

Donncha came to her. ''Where will you go, Mother?''

She looked at the boy. He was fifteen, and like all of Brian's sons, large and strong for his age. ''Where will we go, you mean. I'm not leaving you with Brian, Donncha.''

The lad raised his chin. ''I'm a Dalcassian prince. My father is the High King. I'm not going to leave Kincora. He didn't throw me out. I'm not such a fool as to leave the High King and all he can do for me, to go into exile with you.''

Gormla had taught her son well. She had taught him to be as selfish as she was.

SEVENTEEN

Conspiracy

U pon reaching his stronghold in Leinster, Maelmora sat down to nurse his grudge. The more
he thought about it, the more he decided Brian had
deliberately insulted him. The High King had left
Kincora so as not to be there when Maelmora arrived. And he had surely meant for the prince Murcha to taunt their guest.

"Brian likes to belittle other people," Maelmora
told his Leinstermen. "I have endured it long
enough. I am a King of Leinster. He is only an upstart Dalcassian who seized a crown through brute
force."

When Gormla arrived in Maelmora's hall, she
was even angrier at Brian. Maelmora forgot his
own quarrels with his sister. They had a larger,

common enemy now. They set about planning to get even.

Maelmora enlisted the aid of Sitric Silkbeard. Sitric replied that he was willing to take up arms once more against Brian Boru—provided Maelmora would promise him half the spoils of Munster if they won.

"I always knew I could count on my son," Gormla said smugly.

Maelmora asked, "What about your other son, Donncha? Why didn't you bring him with you?"

Gormla pretended not to hear. She could not bring herself to say that Donncha had deserted her for Brian Boru.

With Gormla gone, Brian should have been able to enjoy a little peace at Kincora, and the company of his children and grandchildren. But he could not. Rumors were soon reaching him about a possible uprising by Leinster and Dublin.

One more time, thought Brian wearily. Is there no end to it?

Leaving Kincora, he made his way up the densely forested slope beyond the outermost walls, climbing ever higher, drawing the sweet air deep into his lungs. Even when the trees blocked his vision, he could still feel the gray crag ahead, waiting for him. In his bones, he felt it.

At last he broke from cover to find himself standing hip deep in heather and bracken, brittle with winter. The ruins of his grandfather's fort lay before him, and above them, Aval's rock. With an effort, he climbed up to it.

Once he could have made the entire climb at a trot without breathing hard. Now his legs were trembling.

I am old, Brian thought. And now I am going to have to fight again after all, or see this land go back to the way it was before. Petty kings squabbling for petty power, tearing each other apart with no sense of the greater good.

Blood and fire, and children crying for their mothers.

Brian stood on the gray crag and looked out across his kingdom. The day was very cold. Once he would not have noticed. Now he shivered, in spite of his great shaggy cloak.

From where he stood he could see the sites of many of his battles. "There we were terribly beaten," he said. "And there we won. In that place a handful of us turned back an army of Ivar's Danes. And on that mountain is buried a company of Leinstermen who defied me. . . ."

He turned slowly, feasting his eyes on hills and meadows, mountains and lake. There was a burning lump in his throat as if he was going to cry, but it had been many years since Brian cried.

The wind blew softly around him, lifting a lock of his silvered hair.

"All that fighting, Aval," Brian murmured to the guardian spirit of the crag. "Yet Ireland is as beautiful as ever. So sweet, so fair . . ."

The lump in his throat was choking him.

"Ahhh, God!" cried Brian Boru, raising his arms pleadingly to the great blue vault of the sky.

Much later, in the twilight, he picked his way carefully down the slope, and ordered the gates of Kincora barred behind him.

Sitric Silkbeard traveled from Dublin to Naas to meet with Maelmora. Gormla insisted on taking part in the meeting. "Take me back to Dublin with you when you go," she told her son. "I don't wish to stay with Maelmora any longer. He sits around talking about attacking Brian, but he won't do it. He is a coward who will not avenge the wrong done me by the High King."

Brian was the second High King to divorce Gormla. Her rage knew no limits.

Sitric told her, "Listen to me, Mother. You shall be avenged. Maelmora and I are going to attack Brian Boru, but we have to wait until we have gathered enough allies. Neither of us wants to be involved in a disaster."

"Brian could die of old age before you do anything!"

"He won't," Sitric assured her. "It is said he can still cut down an opponent in single combat."

"If I had a sword I would cut him down myself," Gormla replied.

She was not a young woman, but the heat of her anger set fire to a beauty not yet faded. Looking at her, Sitric had an idea.

"I'll take you back to Dublin with me," he said.

"But you must remember something. My wife is a daughter of Brian Boru, and the two of you under the one roof will not be easy. I will need your help for a plan I have in mind, but in the meantime, I don't want you making trouble for me in my own hall."

"Me? Make trouble?" Gormla laid one hand on her bosom. "I assure you, I know how to behave. I am a queen!"

Sitric and Maelmora exchanged looks. "I give you credit for being a brave man," the Leinsterman told the Norseman. "I would not care to be under the same roof with my sister and Brian's daughter."

The two men talked together far into the night. Sitric explained his plan for acquiring allies. To this, Gormla listened with interest, her eyes shining. "And remember," Sitric added, "in return for my support I demand half the spoils of Munster. And also, freedom to plunder the entire east coast of Ireland."

This new demand caused Maelmora to scowl. "You ask a lot, Norseman."

"You've just heard my plan for getting us the warriors we need to stand against the might of Brian Boru. And my mother has agreed to it. Take it or leave it, Maelmora."

Maelmora considered. The idea of defeating—and killing—his Munster rival was irresistible. "With Brian dead, this island will be yours and mine to plunder," he said to Sitric Silkbeard.

The agreement was sealed.

Sitric took Gormla back to Dublin with him, and began at once sending messages throughout the Norse trading network.

While they waited for replies, they combined their armies. During the fighting season of the Year of Our Lord 1013, they attacked. Their target was not the High King at Kincora, who was too strong for the number of men they had, but Malachy, in Meath. Malachy's Meathmen were soon hard-pressed by the warriors of Leinster and Dublin. Malachy sent a plea for help to the High King.

When he received this message, Brian knew the time had come.

At the High King's summons, his allies gathered. They included not only many Irish princes, but also Danes from Limerick. "Look at my army, Carroll," Brian said to his historian. "Once I thought the Irish would drive out the Northmen. Now it will be the Irish and Danes fighting the Irish and Norse. Things are never as simple as we would like them to be."

"They are not," Carroll agreed. "Only victory is simple. Everyone understands winning."

"Then pray God we win," said Brian Boru.

He put Murcha in charge of a large force. Murcha's son Turlough was with him, and eager to fight. "All the glory of battle takes place before the fighting," Brian warned him. "You will not find it so pleasant when men are trying to kill you."

But he knew he could not discourage Turlough.

The lad was only fifteen, but there was a light in his eyes that Brian knew.

"I've been teaching my son as you taught me," Murcha told his father. "He will follow me, as I follow you. Your kingdom will be safe with us."

Brian was too deeply moved to answer.

Gormla's son, Donncha, also demanded a company of warriors to lead. He had just reached sword-bearing age, he reminded Brian, and he was keen to see action. But he had had little training for battle. Brian decided to hold him back, to give him some task that would not bring him into the front lines.

As Brian explained to Murcha, "If Donncha has his mother's uncertain temper, he will want seasoning before I use him in an attack."

Murcha was pleased that Brian had no such reservations about Turlough.

The High King marched east. The summer was spent putting down a number of small tribes that were loyal to Maelmora. Then Brian marched on to Dublin to face Sitric Silkbeard.

Brian's advance had drawn Sitric's warriors away from Meath, but they left Malachy's army so badly mauled it was not much help to the High King. Without them, Brian laid siege to Dublin. His daughter and Gormla watched from the walls, each thinking her own thoughts.

Sitric had his stronghold well fortified, however, and in the end Brian withdrew the siege. The weather had turned against him; it was time for the warriors to go home, to rest and repair their weapons.

There would be another fighting season next year.

"By next year," Brian said to Murcha, "Malachy should have rebuilt his army, and will be able to join us."

As soon as the siege was lifted, Sitric Silkbeard left Dublin on a fast boat. The sea that autumn was wild and rough but Sitric had Viking blood. He stood in the prow, just behind the dragon head, and laughed at the salt spray.

Sitric was welcomed like a blood brother into the Viking hall of Sigurd the Stout, Earl of Orkney. Like many of the Norsemen who lived beyond the shores of Ireland, Sigurd had watched with interest Brian Boru's rise to power. He had seen the Dalcassian turn a tangle of warring tribes into one people, wealthy and well armed, and perhaps too strong to be plundered by Vikings any longer. Sigurd had not approved of this turn of events. Ireland had long been a rich source of gold and slaves and timber, a source he was sorry to lose.

Now Sitric Silkbeard was offering him a chance to help destroy Brian. But Sigurd of Orkney was no fool. He had heard enough stories about Brian Boru to make him cautious.

It had taken something unusual to tempt him. His reply to Sitric's message had been an invitation to Orkney to discuss the matter further.

As they sat together in the hall, drinking from

huge horns filled with Danish beer, Sigurd said, "Tell me again what special prize you offer me, in return for my support."

"I offer you the most beautiful woman who ever combed her hair."

"That is what you said in your message. But I wanted to see you, man to man, before I agreed. You would not lie to me? You can actually give me such a woman?"

"I can," Sitric assured him. "She is my mother, the Princess Gormla."

Sigurd of Orkney licked his lips. He was a massive mountain of flesh—like some big hog waiting to be roasted, Sitric thought with distaste. But he commanded many Viking warriors.

"I've heard of this woman," Sigurd said. "The Norse sagasingers praise her beauty."

"She was once wife to Olaf Cuaran, the Norse King of Dublin. My father," Sitric added. "And now I am willing to see her married to you, if you will help me destroy the Irish High King."

Sigurd licked his thick lips again. "A woman like that makes a man famous. I would not mind having her. But when we win, I also demand the plunder of the north half of Ireland!"

"Done," agreed Sitric Silkbeard.

With the Vikings of Orkney as allies, the army of Sitric and Maelmora would be much stronger. But Sitric, too, had become a cautious man when it came to Brian Boru. He wanted to be sure of even more warriors before he faced the High King across a battlefield.

Using Gormla as bait had worked well with Sigurd of Orkney, so her son planned to use her again. When he left Orkney he set sail for the Isle of Man. There he met two brothers, Ospak and Brodir, who ruled that island. These Viking brothers had thirty ships between them and a mighty reputation for savagery.

When Sitric's boat put into harbor on the Isle of Man, a seaman told the King of Dublin a strange story. "Brodir was raised as a Christian," the man claimed, "but he has converted to paganism. His soul is twice blackened."

"Brodir sounds like the very man I need," said Sitric Silkbeard.

By the time he at last returned to Dublin, Sitric was able to report to Gormla, and to Maelmora, that they now had enough powerful allies to destroy Brian. "At my summons, I can bring a thousand Viking ships to Dublin, packed with warriors howling for Brian's blood. Perhaps there is no man in Ireland who can defeat the High King, but I have found men elsewhere who are eager to do so."

In private, Gormla asked her son, "Did you promise me to Sigurd?"

"I did."

"And this Brodir . . . did you also promise me to him?"

"I did. He said he would not join us unless I gave him whatever I gave Sigurd. But the fighting will be savage. With any luck, both men will be killed and neither will claim you.''

"I just want to be certain Brian Boru is killed," said Gormla. She could not bear it that a man so splendid—a man she had once desired above any other—had rejected her.

In Munster there was great surprise when a dragonship flying a foreign flag sailed up the Shannon. For many years, Brian had kept the river free of Viking warcraft. When the vessel was beached below Kincora, Brian went to meet it with a party of Dalcassian warriors.

The man in command of the boat announced himself as Ospak, of the Isle of Man. "I have come this long way to warn you," he told Brian. "My brother Brodir plans to make war on you. I said nothing when he turned his back on Christianity, but I cannot go along with him now. I know you for a good king, Brian Boru. You have treated even your enemies fairly. I tell you this: my brother schemes with the rulers of Dublin and Leinster to kill you. He has been promised your former wife as a prize of war."

For a moment, Brian almost laughed. "He would be getting what he deserves," he started to say—then he remembered Gormla as she had been when he first saw her, as beautiful as Ireland. He bit back the words.

Brian made Ospak welcome in the feasting hall at Kincora. There he heard the details of the plot against him.

"Sigurd of Orkney is sending ships and men," Ospak told Brian. "And there are others interested as well. Amlaff of Denmark plans to claim a share of the spoils in return for giving Sitric warriors. Norsemen are also coming from Scotland, the Shetland Islands, and the Hebrides."

"So Sitric and Maelmora think it will take a huge army to kill me?" said Brian. "I am flattered."

"Do not jest about your death," said Murcha.

Brian turned toward his son. "People have been trying to kill me for as long as I can remember. I don't take that threat seriously anymore. The threat to plunder Ireland, though . . . I take that very seriously. It shall not happen. Not while my strong hand is uppermost." He looked at Murcha, and beyond him, to young Turlough, being trained to follow his father and grandfather. Brian's voice rang strong in the feasting hall. His face was lined, his hair was gray, but his eyes were clear and hard. All his life was in them. He did not mean to be defeated.

Swiftly he sent messengers of his own, seeking allies. Ospak carried word to Prince Malcolm of Scotland, who had married another of Brian's daughters. Malcolm promised to send a band of warriors led by the Steward of Mar.

Young Donncha kept pleading to take part in the battle to come. Brian still did not trust him for the front lines. Instead, he said, "You may take a picked company of horsemen down toward Waterford. Keep the Vikings in that area distracted, so they do not come up to Dublin.''

''I want to take part in the real war,'' protested Donncha.

''It is all war,'' his father told him. ''You can get killed as easily in one place as in another. Do as I command. That's the way you can be of the most help to me.''

Donncha obeyed, though not with good grace. ''You're favoring Turlough mac Murcha over me,'' he complained.

The winter passed, the fighting season approached. When his army was gathered around Kincora, Brian rode among the men on his favorite gray horse. The warriors were eager to be on the march, but he held them back with the force of his will until he was certain everything was ready. The smallest detail did not escape him. Nothing could be half done, or half ready. With a keen eye, he examined the fitness of the men, the sea of spears and pikes they carried, the gleam of sword and shortsword, the deadly edges of the axes.

As always, the warriors were divided by tribes. Each group was clustered around the standard of its leader. Brian rode over to where Carroll the historian was watching. ''See that, Carroll? One of those standards belongs to the Danes of Limerick. Mark it well.''

When at last Brian was satisfied that the men were ready, he gave the order to march.

He looked back only once. After they had

crossed the Shannon, he reined in his horse and turned to gaze for a long time toward Kincora, and the gray crag.

Then he set his face toward Dublin and urged the horse forward.

EIGHTEEN

Preparing for Battle

In the Year of Our Lord 1014, spring came early to Ireland. As Brian led his army through the countryside, grass was greening and lambs bloomed like flowers on the hillsides.

Shortly before Palm Sunday, Sitric's foreign allies began arriving in Dublin. At first there was only one longship, then two, but they were the advance wave of hundreds. Sitric welcomed them gladly. There was no doubt a great battle would soon take place.

According to the historians who would write of the battle afterward, the foreigners brought with them as many as one thousand coats of chain mail. So much armor, so many weapons, so many warriors hoping to defeat Brian Boru!

Maelmora reached Dublin at the head of his army of Leinstermen. He told Sitric, "Malachy is on the march, but still some distance away. In order to reward his Meathmen, he's letting them plunder the land north of the Liffey."

Sitric scowled. "I promised the plunder of that region to our own allies."

"Then let us attack Malachy and stop him!"

"First, I want to know how near the High King is," said Sitric.

The scouts he sent out soon reported, "The army of the High King has caught up with Malachy. There was some argument about the plundering. Brian Boru was said to be angry about it. Perhaps he wanted it for himself, or his own men. We do not know. But the armies are together now, under his command."

Sitric gnawed his lip. He would have preferred to attack Brian and Malachy separately. But if the two had united, there was nothing for it but to fight them together.

"I'm thankful we have so many coming to help us," he told Maelmora. They went together to stand on the walls of Dublin and watch Viking longships coming in to harborage.

Meanwhile, Brian was calling a council of war. Foremost among them was Murcha, and his cousin Conaing, one of Brian's most trusted warriors. The leather command tent was crowded with hard-faced men who held the light of battle in their eyes.

The sentry at the tent flap refused to let Turlough

mac Murcha enter. "You are too young, lad."

"My father is in there, and my grandfather. And I am not too young to die with them." Turlough drew himself up proudly.

The sentry would recall those words later.

He drew back the flap. "Enter, then."

Turlough was fifteen years old. Most men did not become warriors until they were sixteen, and he was aware of the honor he had been given and determined to make Brian and Murcha proud of him. He was certain nothing as exciting as this moment had ever happened before. He slipped into the tent and flattened himself against the wall, hardly daring to breathe lest someone notice him and make him leave.

Malachy was protesting the fact that Ospak of Man was included in Brian's army. "I think he's a spy," Malachy said. "I don't want him with us."

"He has proved himself a friend and an ally," Brian replied.

"But he's a foreigner!"

"Many of those we once called foreigners are marching with me," Brian said in his deep, slow voice. "They are part of the Irish army now. I have treated them firmly but fairly, and we know what to expect of each other. I can turn my unshielded back to them without fear."

"I don't see things the way you do at all," Malachy said.

Brian nodded gravely. "I know that. I hope in time to be able to change your mind."

But as the discussion went on, Brian and Malachy disagreed more and more. Malachy did not approve of any of Brian's battle plans. When Brian spoke of moving men in this way and that to trap the enemy, Malachy refused. "If we just run at them all at once and overpower them, the battle will soon be over," he insisted.

Murcha could not hold his temper any longer. "Don't you know how many warriors Sitric and Maelmora are bringing in? They will be spread out for miles along the coast. We can't fight them in the old way. My father's way is the only plan that can work. He is the High King, Malachy, and you must remember that. The command decisions are his to make. He knows better than you do."

The Meath king was offended. "I have won many battles," he said coldly. "And I was not trying to steal another man's authority, if that's what you're accusing me of. That is not my way."

Murcha reddened. "If you mean that as an insult to my father, take it back."

"Murcha!" said Brian warningly.

Malachy growled, "Apologize for your son, Brian. He is a discredit to you."

Everyone looked at Brian, but Brian was looking at Murcha. To the younger man's surprise, he said softly, "Murcha is a great credit to me, and I shall never apologize for him. He is loyal to me, so I am loyal to him."

For a heartbeat it seemed as if there was no one in the tent but Brian and Murcha, who gave his father a look of such love and gratitude it made Brian's eyes sting.

Malachy said angrily, "If you place Murcha above me you do not need me, or my men." He whirled around and left the tent, almost knocking Turlough aside on his way.

Murcha said to his father, "I'm sorry. My temper has cost you another ally. I always seem to say the wrong thing at the wrong time."

Brian smiled. "If you know that much, you are making progress. Let it be, Murcha. The battle draws near and we are all tense. When Malachy has had time to think, he will come back to us. He has a good heart in him."

As Murcha started to leave the tent, he saw Turlough. "What are you doing here?" he asked his son.

"Learning," the lad replied truthfully.

Murcha clapped him on the shoulder. "Come with me, then. The lessons will soon begin in earnest."

Brian had long made it a habit to hold back from battle until he was in a superior position and could be certain of winning. But this time, much was against him. He had lost, at least for a while, the support of Malachy and his Meathmen. Also, the land around Dublin favored the defenders, whose numbers were constantly increasing. By the day before Good Friday, Sitric's harbor was filled with ships. The singing and shouting of the Vikings rang out clearly in the evening air, carrying as far as Brian's encampment to the west.

Brian stood outside his tent, listening. He became aware of Murcha at his shoulder. "When we set out from Kincora, I was certain of superior numbers," he said to his son. "Now I'm not so sure. And I'm weary."

It was the first time Murcha had heard his father admit to any form of weakness. "If you're weary, Father, you can lean on me."

Brian turned and smiled at him. "I'm not too weary for what must be done. We cannot simply march back to Munster and leave the land to her enemies. We have to fight. And it is better that we fight tomorrow than wait any longer. If we delay, the battle might be joined on Easter Sunday. I refuse to kill anyone on that holy day."

Murcha looked at Brian's silver hair and stooping shoulders. The weight of seventy-three years was pressing down on the High King. Last year he had still been able to use his sword, but this was a new fighting season, and would be a terrible battle.

When Brian said, "We shall march at dawn," Murcha argued with his father one last time.

"You must not take an active part in the battle," he said to Brian. "You are the heart and soul of our people. If anything should happen to you . . ." Murcha could not finish that thought. Instead he said, "Give me your sword, Father, and let me lead the army tomorrow in your name, following your battle plans. I have done much that has hurt you.

Let me make it up to you now, this way.

"You were right all along, I see that now. I should have listened to you. I will listen, in the future. Just promise me you will be in my future! Keep yourself safe while I defeat Sitric and Maelmora in the name of the High King. The Emperor of the Irish," he added. Carroll had told him of the words in the Book of Armagh.

Brian could not speak. He put one arm around Murcha's shoulders and hugged hard.

Murcha's heart leaped. Why did I not admit to him long ago that I knew I was wrong? he wondered. It was so easy, it just took a few words. Now those words have built a bridge between us.

At last Brian said, "Leave me my sword tomorrow. I have carried it for too long to surrender it to anyone, even you. But you may take the command. I shall wait at a safe distance and pray for your victory."

Alone in his tent that night, with his attendant Laiten standing guard outside, Brian tried to sleep. The night before a battle was always difficult. His brain imagined the day to come, going over and over it and allowing him no rest. He sighed. He tossed. Several times he got up and went to the entrance of the tent.

Each time he found Laiten awake. "Do you wish anything?" the faithful man would ask.

"Nothing," Brian replied. He lay back down on the ground again and rolled himself in his cloak, as he had for so long, before so many battles.

Shortly before dawn, he saw a faint glow. There was no torch and no fire in the tent, and it was still too early for dawn light. Brian sat up, peering toward the mysterious glow.

"Aval?" he whispered.

Men everywhere saw visions that night. Some claimed to have heard the wail of a banshee. A group of Brian's enemies, encamped on the beach, told of seeing a figure on a gray horse, a ghostly shape they took to mean their own doom. They fled, howling with fear.

Others claimed the same vision promised them victory. Brodir of Man boasted that the specter had promised him the destruction of Brian Boru.

Brian's son Murcha saw something that night, but he would not speak of it. Turlough glimpsed a wild, strange look of joy and despair mingled in his father's eyes, however, and was afraid.

All men were glad when Good Friday finally dawned, chasing away the spirits of the night.

NINETEEN

The Battle of Clontarf

D awn, the twenty-third day of April, in the Year
of Our Lord 1014. A clear dawn, with only a
few tattered rags of cloud in the sky, streaming
across the face of the rising sun.

The High King's command tent was pitched in
Tomar's Wood, overlooking an area that would see
much of the fighting. From the timbered palisade
of Dublin, Sitric and his wife and mother had another vantage point. Sitric had chosen not to take
part personally in the battle, but had not bothered to
inform Maelmora of his decision.

Sitric had met Brian Boru on the battlefield
before. He was not anxious to repeat the experience.

In Tomar's Wood, Brian emerged from his tent

to address his warriors before they went to battle. A great cheer went up when they saw him. Murcha had gathered the Dalcassians in the forefront. Brian called many of them by name, praising their courage. As he spoke, many men wept. Brian knew how to touch their hearts.

The sight of the High King inspired his followers as nothing else could. He was Brian Boru, and they were going out to fight and perhaps die for him.

Murcha led the Dalcassians. Cian, son of Molloy, led the Owenachts, once enemies to the Dalcassians. They were enemies no longer. With the Danes of Limerick, they were simply "the Irish" now.

They were the warriors of Brian Boru.

The order to march was given, and they moved out, following Murcha's standard. According to the bards, Murcha mac Brian was the last man in Ireland trained to use both his right and his left hand equally in wielding weapons. This he had learned from Brian Boru.

Close to his shoulder was his son Turlough, who was being prepared in all ways to succeed him.

The army of the High King marched bravely and haughtily, with one mind.

The enemy prepared to meet them. The ranks of Maelmora's Leinstermen were swelled by Sitric's Norsemen. But the most fearsome warriors of all were those who came leaping out of the longships and wading ashore through the shallows, screaming for blood. They had come without honor and without mercy. They had come to plunder, come to kill.

In addition to swords and axes they had polished yellow bows, and quivers filled with arrows. Some had dragons and snakes painted on their flesh. Some were berserkers, men dressed in bearskins and out of their minds with drugged wine.

Holding his men back, Malachy of Meath watched from a distant hill. "Let Brian Boru do it without me," he said, standing with folded arms.

The two armies came together with a mighty impact, shield to shield and breast to breast, eye glaring into angry eye. A thousand screams of fury split the air at once.

Young Turlough had not expected such total confusion. One moment there were two masses of men. The next moment there was only one mass of shouting, slashing, cursing warriors locked in combat. Soon they were so covered in blood you could not tell one from another.

Turlough dodged, ran, struck, dodged again, always moving forward, trying to keep his eye on his father's standard so he would not be separated from the Dalcassians. He did not have time to be afraid; everything was happening too fast.

From the walls of Dublin, Brian's daughter Emer thought she could see the standard of the three lions and cried out, "Brian Boru!"

Sitric snarled at her, "Cheer for my side, wife."

She gave him a hostile stare. "My father is an old man, yet he goes to war. You are a young man, yet you stand here with the women.''

"Maelmora's down there somewhere. If he's killed, who would be in command? I have to protect myself in case I am needed later.''

Emer snorted.

Gormla, who was standing just beyond Sitric, said nothing at all. She was shading her eyes with her hand, trying to make out the standard of Maelmora of Leinster.

Following Brian's battle plan, once they met the enemy his warriors formed themselves into three lines, attempting to pin the foreigners between them. But led by Sigurd and Brodir, the enemy was also using a plan. They were fighting for time while they waited for the last men off the ships to join them. The invaders had been coming ashore since sunrise, when the tide was full and the vessels could come close to land.

Maelmora of Leinster was unaware that Sitric Silkbeard was not also in the field. As he hewed and hacked his way through men, he was looking for Sitric. Perhaps that is why he did not see Conaing the Dalcassian until it was too late.

Brian's nephew had just slain one of the warriors from Orkney and was turning to meet a new challenge when he found himself face to face with the King of Leinster. They had last seen each other at the ill-fated chess game in the hall at Kincora. Conaing grinned a savage grin. "There's no yew tree for you to hide in here, Maelmora!'' he cried, leaping at his foe.

Watching from the walls of Dublin, Gormla had just caught sight of her brother's standard when she saw it fall. Next she glimpsed the standard of Conaing of the Dalcassians. Then it too fell, and was seen no more.

Gormla drew in a deep breath. Without turning to look at Sitric, she asked, "Have you brought in enough foreigners to kill Brian Boru even without my brother's help?"

"Why?"

Gormla did not answer. She kept her eyes on the battle, and her fists clenched.

Dublin, the town of the black pool, occupied the land south of the Liffey. The area north of the river was now fully overrun by warriors. Smoke was rising from various outlying districts that had been burned in the march to battle.

The only way to reach Dublin from the battlefield was by Dugall's Bridge. The fighting was heavy there throughout the day. It was also heavy around a fishing weir on the river Tolka, a place that would come to be known as the Weir of Clontarf.

Sitric's army, for the most part, fought with their backs to the sea that had brought them. Brian's men fought with their backs to the land that was theirs.

Because the day was Good Friday, those who were Christians in Dublin—and there were many of them—sought to observe the holy day. It was impossible. The fighting was too near. Prayers could not be heard above the shrieks of the dying.

At Brian's order, his men marked out for special attack the invaders who wore coats of mail. With the axes Brian had taught them to use, the Irish cut the armor to bits.

Watching from the walls, Sitric at first compared the scene to that of reapers cutting corn in a field. "See how my men are flinging the sheaves to the ground," he boasted.

Emer replied, "The true harvest will be measured at the end of the day."

Gormla said nothing. She stared grimly toward the battle, wondering where Brian was.

Was he alive? Or dead?

Did she really want him dead?

Did she really want to be carried away to Orkney, or the Isle of Man, to end her days in a foreign hall as the wife of a brutal man?

How had things come to this? she wondered.

The day was long and terrible. The tide turned and still the fighting went on. And still Malachy watched from his hill.

Murcha was fighting like a man inspired. No one could stand against him. He cut his way through the enemy ranks with his brave young son beside him until he reached the Earl of Orkney himself, Sigurd the Stout.

Sigurd's raven banner identified the man, and was a rallying point for his followers. Murcha quickly killed the standard bearer so the Orkney warlord's position would not be known by his men. Alarmed, Sigurd shouted for someone else to lift the standard, but the man he had thought his most trusted friend cried, "Carry it yourself!" and fled.

Murcha mac Brian was a terrifying sight on that day. No one wanted to face him.

Sigurd, abandoned, had no choice.

With a right-handed blow, Murcha hit Sigurd's head so hard that the Orkneyman's helmet straps burst and the bronze helmet flew from his head. A heartbeat later Murcha's left hand drove a sword deep into Sigurd's body, and the Earl of Orkney was dead.

Murcha turned and began fighting his way toward the Weir of Clontarf, where a number of Dalcassians had engaged the enemy in the most savage fighting of the day.

By this time, everyone in Dublin was trying to find a place on the walls from which to watch the fighting. They saw the tide of battle move back and forth for a long time, but at last it became clear that the High King's forces were winning.

A light came into Emer's eyes. Her husband Sitric wore a face like a winter storm.

Gormla merely stood and stared.

Toward evening Brian's forces made a combined and very determined attack, and the enemy fell back at every point. Soon they were running, with the High King's army in hot pursuit.

At that point, as the watchers on the wall noted, Malachy changed his mind. He and his Meathmen hurried to join the fight. They mingled with Brian's men, sharing in the final slaughter.

In terror, the invaders ran for the ships that had brought them.

Emer cried triumphantly, "Your foreigners rush to claim their inheritance, the sea! They gallop over the plain like a herd of cattle driven mad by flies!" She laughed with joy.

Enraged, Sitric struck the daughter of Brian Boru such a blow that he broke two of her teeth.

But Emer did not cry.

Murcha was so weary he could hardly lift his arms to strike another blow, but he could not stop fighting until the last of the enemy surrendered or was dead. He saw yet another foreign banner in the distance and hurried toward it, sword in hand.

In the tent in Tomar's Wood, Brian had waited through the long day for each bit of news from the battle. Again and again he sent Laiten to observe and report. "Can you still see my son's standard?" the High King would ask eagerly.

"I can," came the answer.

"Then all is well."

But soon Brian would ask again, "Can you still see my son's standard?"

"I can. The fighting is so heavy it sounds as if a huge crowd is cutting down the forest with axes. But there is the banner of Murcha mac Brian, and it is moving forward."

Brian managed a faint smile.

The third time he asked the question was late in the day. Twilight, blue and shadowed, was creeping through Tomar's Wood. The sounds of battle had grown fainter, for fewer men were alive to fight. The High King's forces were driving the enemy ahead of them into the sea.

The tide, which had been full at sunrise, was full again at sunset. The foreigners were drowning in the water that had carried them to Ireland.

"Where is Murcha's banner now?" Brian called to Laiten, who had climbed a tree to have a better view.

"I see it . . . there . . . I . . . it is fallen."

Brian stopped breathing. "Fallen?"

"The Prince Murcha has fallen also," Laiten said sorrowfully. "He does not rise."

Brian stood at the entrance to his tent, listening to the fading sounds of battle. The last battle sounds I shall ever hear, he thought. And the enemy is defeated.

"Is my son dead?" he forced himself to ask Laiten. "Go and see." But he did not have to wait for the answer. He knew it in his heart. Aval had told him.

Brian Boru had taken many blows in his long life. He took this as he had taken the others, standing.

His enemies were crushed. They had swam against the tide, they had attacked a mighty oak with their puny fists. They had flung themselves against a will stronger than their own, and had been broken. Now they lay bloody and uncaring on the battlefield, or floated on the swelling tide, their dreams of plunder forgotten.

But they had not died alone. Though every foreign leader, except Brodir of Man, had been killed in the day's fighting, many Irish princes were also dead. In slaying Maelmora of Leinster, Conaing the Dalcassian had lost his life.

Murcha, son and Tanist of Brian Boru, the man trained to preserve Brian's vision of kingship, had died at the very close of battle.

And in the bloody waters of the Weir of Clontarf, with his fingers still tangled in the yellow hair of the Viking he had killed there, young Turlough mac Murcha floated with his dead face turned toward the sky.

A kind fate spared Brian this final heartbreak.

As he stood in the twilight, Brodir of Man was running wildly through Tomar's Wood, trying to hide from pursuing Dalcassians. He was the last invading warlord left alive.

Soon Brodir, mad with fear, would stumble across a leather tent and a tall, white-haired old man who still had his sword.

Neither would live to see the first star.

But Brian did not know this as he stood listening to the last sounds of battle. He knew only that Murcha was dead, and that his army had won a mighty victory. Never again would the Vikings try to take Ireland by force. The plunderers were dead. The survivors would become "the Irish."

Already, Brian could hear his men beginning to celebrate. Down by the shore, the army of the High King was chanting its victory cry. The voices of the

Gael mingled with those of Brian's loyal Danes, rising to make one voice, one clear cry of triumph.

"Boru! BORU! *BORU!*"

Listening, Brian Boru smiled through his tears.

Available by mail from  **TOR** **FORGE®**
FORGE **TOR®**

CHICAGO BLUES • Hugh Holton
Police Commander Larry Cole returns in his most dangerous case to date when he investigates the murders of two assassins that bear the same M.O. as long-ago, savage, vigilante cases.

KILLER.APP • Barbara D'Amato
"Dazzling in its complexity and chilling in its exposure of how little privacy anyone has…totally mesmerizing."—*Cleveland Plain Dealer*

CAT IN A DIAMOND DAZZLE • Carole Nelson Douglas
The fifth title in Carole Nelson Douglas's Midnight Louie series—"All ailurphiles addicted to Lilian Jackson Braun's "The Cat Who…" mysteries…can latch onto a new *puri*vate eye: Midnight Louie—slinking and sleuthing on his own, a la Mike Hammer."—*Fort Worth Star Telegram*

STRONG AS DEATH • Sharan Newman
The fourth title in Sharan Newman's critically acclaimed Catherine LeVendeur mystery series pits Catherine and her husband in a bizarre game of chance—which may end in Catherine's death.

PLAY IT AGAIN • Stephen Humphrey Bogart
In the classic style of a Bogart and Bacall movie, Stephen Humphrey Bogart delivers a gripping, fast-paced mystery."—*Baltimore Sun*

BLACKENING SONG • Aimée and David Thurlo
The first novel in the Ella Clah series involving ex-FBI agent, Ella Clah, investigating murders on a Navajo Reservation.

Call toll-free 1-800-288-2131 to use your major credit card or clip and mail this form below to order by mail

- ✂

Send to: Publishers Book and Audio Mailing Service
PO Box 120159, Staten Island, NY 10312-0004

☐ 54464-1 **Chicago Blues** ....$5.99/$7.99 ☐ 53935-4 **Strong as Death** ....$5.99/$7.99
☐ 55391-8 **Killer.App** ....$5.99/$7.99 ☐ 55162-1 **Play It Again** ....$5.99/$6.99
☐ 55506-6 **Cat in a Diamond Dazzle** ....$6.99/$8.99 ☐ 56756-0 **Blackening Song** ....$5.99/$7.99

Please send me the following books checked above. I am enclosing $_____. (Please add $1.50 for the first book, and 50¢ for each additional book to cover postage and handling. Send check or money order only—no CODs).

Name _____

Address _____ **City** _____ **State** _____ **Zip** _____